Journeys of The Dublin Trio II

by

Dan McMeans

To my three beautiful daughters, who were a joy to raise and who have transitioned into wonderful adult women and mothers, who carry themselves with much dignity and maturity. They make me proud every day, and I love them without limits.

"Journeys of The Dublin Trio II," by Dan McMeans ISBN 978-1-63868-229-5 (softcover).

Published 2025 by Virtualbookworm.com Publishing, P.O. Box 9949, College Station, TX 77842, US.

Contents

The Haunted House

A group of ten teenagers, five girls and five boys, lost a bet with another group of teens. That meant they had to spend a weekend at a notorious haunted house in the neighborhood. Upon arriving at the haunted house, the group found it surrounded by a tall metal fence that they had to climb over. First, the guys helped the girls climb over the fence, and then the boys followed suit. After entering the property, they were able to get a closer look at the house. To them, it was gothic-looking and very creepy, since it was 300 years old. Nevertheless, the teens proceeded forward and entered the house. Once in, they turned on their flashlights and moved beyond the foyer. As they walked around the house, they noticed that the house had a central fireplace made of brick, dual staircases, wooden ceiling beams above, floors made of broad planks, and intricate molding.

As the teenagers walked through the house, they found it fascinating. Then, the group came across five portraits of family members who had lived in the house. Each picture had a name and the year it was painted. These paintings were between 250 to 300 years old. The boys were goofing off as they looked at the portraits, but the girls were amazed at how lifelike the portraits were. It was time for dinner, and the group decided to make a homemade turkey dinner with all the fixings. The girls went to the supermarket to purchase a turkey and the fixings, then brought them back to the house to cook. The kitchen had an old-fashioned fireplace with suspended pots. These were key to cooking during colonial times, since they allowed cooks to swing pots and kettles over the fire, providing temperature control. The group enjoyed a traditional feast prepared by the girls. Afterward, they turned in for the night. This old house had five bedrooms, so each bunked up for the night.

While they were sleeping, they heard something metallic marching up and down the hallway. It sounded very creepy, so the boys told the girls to stay in their rooms while they investigated the noise. They found, to their horror, a life-size suit of armor from medieval times walking up and down the hallway. The hallway walls displayed swords from that time period, which the boys grabbed to fend off the spirit in a suit of armor. Still, the suit of armor was well-versed in sword fighting and was able to defend itself against the boys. Eventually, the boys gained momentum and cornered the spirit until they saw it leave the suit of armor. The boys followed the spirit down the stairs until it vanished into one of the portraits. The girls came down the steps to discuss what had just happened, and now they believe ghosts are associated with the portraits, but why?

The group thought this issue was too big for them. One of the boys recalls an ad featuring a former Green Beret who offered help in solving problems where people had lost hope, and also assisted with matters in the mystical realm. He Googled his name to see if he would be of help and then contacted him. The Dublin Trio arrived, and the group told him about what had happened. The Trio approaches the portrait in question and looks at the year it was painted, which was 1724. He looked at the name of the person in the portrait, which was Sir Nicolas Bevenloth. The Trio was curious if there was anything behind the picture. He looked and, sure enough, there was a safe behind the portrait. The safe had a lock that was opened with a key. The Dublin Trio was skilled in picking locks, and he was able to unlock the safe, only to find a diary.

In the diary, Sir Nicolas recounts his struggles with his wife's faith and her nobility. Hence, he prayed to Satan to help him torture his wife, but she was firm in her faith, so it didn't work. Sir Nicolas then asked Satan for more evil. Satan allowed him access to other evil entities in the universe besides Satan that Sir Nicolas could utilize to torture his wife. His wife was afflicted by a tremendous malevolent energy. Still, she was resilient and had a strong moral compass to guide her, drawing on prayers and the timeless passage of God's words that humanity must find a way to overcome evil. With those things, she got stronger in spirit and was infused by God to fight off the infliction from her husband. She was defiant to the end of her life. Still, the evil spirit lives on in the portrait, and now these teenagers must deal with it.

Suddenly, a ghost appeared, descending the steps with a laugh, and held his head in his hands. It was creepy. The ghost, dressed in 17th-century attire, was walking around the teens. The Dublin Trio stood in the ghost's path, and the ghost returned to the portrait, but before he did, he looked back at the Dublin Trio as if to say, "I'll remember you".

The Dublin Trio slept on the couch in the living room that night, and he was roused awake by what he thought was the sound of things moving around in the living room. He found a seven-foot statue that was in the living room. It was originally in the corner, but now it wasn't in the corner. It was approximately eight feet from where he was sleeping. He found it startling and worrisome that this had happened, so he called the group downstairs to discuss the situation. When the group arrived, the statue began to move its limbs with fluidity, as if its stone body had come to life.

It grabbed one of the girls and started to do twirls with her forcefully, and made her dance with him as he twirled her and dipped her against her will. This sickened the Dublin Trio, so he ran out to the shed and grabbed a sledgehammer. He ran back and took a whack at the statue's legs, and took off a big part of the statue beneath its right leg. The statue responded with a turnaround right cross, but the Trio ducked. The Trio took the sledgehammer and whacked the statue against the left hip, taking out a chunk of the left hip, which caused the statue to be off kilter. The Dublin Trio then gave the statue a karate kick in the midsection, causing it to land on its back. The Trio struck one final blow to the statue's head, and afterward, everyone witnessed the evil spirit depart the statue's stone body. It started to mock the teenagers and the Trio.

"You will end up enslaved upstairs, in the lost spirit room," said the spirit. The Dublin Trio replied: "In the power that's in my God, I rebuke you and break any curses, hexes, spells, and demonic activity or any other evil thing that has been sent against us and let them return to their origins defeated." Soon, white particles came out of thin air, bound the evil spirit, and dragged him back to his portrait, where he will rest in peace forever.

The Dublin Trio and the teenagers were perplexed by the spirit's words about the lost spirit room, so they went upstairs and found a locked room. The Trio kicked the door down, and to their astonishment, they found luminous white spirits, each about the size of a softball, that had been trapped in this room by the evil ghost. The spirits recognized their freedom and walked through the doorway's threshold as if they were becoming humanized. As they walked down the hallway, a luminous light appeared from the far corner, growing bigger and wider. The good ghostly figures stepped into the light. The light welcomed them home, one by one. The group watched in wonder and amazement how all things seem to come together for the better when you care and put in the time. They thought of how the situation happened because they lost a bet. Think of all the matters that can come out for the best when you maintain hope for a better tomorrow.

The Dublin Trio Meets Thor

The Greek gods known as the Olympians were growing increasingly concerned about the greenhouse gases warming the Earth and causing climate change. This affected their environment on Mount Olympus. They knew that evil was behind the Earth's warming up and causing devastation. Two gods from Mount Olympus, Zeus and Poseidon, wanted to help. So, they sent down to Earth a courageous protector of humanity--Thor.

Before taking this step, they needed to notify the person they wanted Thor to work with to correct the problem. After reviewing numerous individuals, they selected the Dublin Trio to collaborate with Thor. They notified the Dublin Trio from Mount Olympus by faxing him. They used space-time continuum mechanics to send the fax. This is a framework in physics that combines space and time into a single four-dimensional entity, allowing objects to move. The Dublin Trio was outside, watering his flower beds, when the fax arrived. What people don't know about the Dublin Trio is that while his martial art skills can be lethal, he is also a gentle man who appreciates the finer elements of life.

He goes into his house to check the fax machine, and the message says, "This message is about the utmost global proportions. If you accept this mission, please arrange to meet me at the Friendly Pub at Hendrick St and Bustle Ave. I'll be wearing a gray raincoat, so you'll be able to identify me. I'll be able to go into more detail about what this mission is all about when we meet." The Dublin Trio was puzzled as to what this meant. Still, he felt obligated to go since it was based on global proportions, so he went to the pub. He saw the man with the gray raincoat at the bar. They sat down and talked. The man with the gray raincoat said that his family has been observing Earth for some time now. They know that the Earth is in trouble with the planet warming up, causing catastrophic changes throughout the world and his family wants to help. "Who is your family?" The Dublin Trio asked.

The man in the raincoat told the Dublin Trio to try to understand mythology and folklore. He said you must have heard about the Greek gods who live on Mount Olympus, the highest mountain in Greece. They care deeply for humanity. He informed the Dublin Trio that he is part of a family selected to help mitigate the effects of global warming on Earth.

"My name is Thor," "I'm in alliance with the Greek Gods, but I'm from the Norse affiliation. We all work together to protect humanity. I didn't bring my hammer with me because it would be too hard to conceal while getting around. Here's the situation: Satan is using an old mine shaft to resonate his evil energy to the planet Venus. Emeralds on Venus are used to augment a tower of evil terror and beam it back to Earth to warm Earth's atmosphere. This is done because Satan hates all of creation, and we need you to team up with us to stop this evil resonance from the mine shaft."

Thor continued. "The sooner we get to work, the better. The mine shaft is heavily guarded, but I believe we can take them. The abandoned mine is called the Rittenhouse Gap Mine, and it is located in Berks County, Pennsylvania."

"I've heard much folklore about the Greek gods," said The Dublin Trio. "But I had no idea they were real. Of course, whatever I can do to assist you, you can count on me."

"I must warn you about what you might be up against," said Thor. "Satan is very deceitful. He will lie to gain any advantage he can get. He can imitate any voice from your past, including your mom's. There is no method beneath his evilness that he won't use to gain an advantage. I'm talking about pure evil of the worst kind. That means your concentration and discipline must be at their peak performance."

"Let's get down to work." The Trio said.

The next morning, Thor and the Dublin Trio drive out to Berks County, which is a six-hour drive from Philadelphia. Once in Berks County, they go straight to the Rittenhouse Gap Mine and get right to work. They found an entryway into the mine shaft and slowly walked down the mine corridor. They knew their mission as they walked deeper into the mine shaft. Out of the blue, a wooden door appeared before them. This really perplexed them as they stood thinking, wondering why a wooden door would appear out of nowhere in the mine shaft.

Suddenly, they heard a voice call out in the mine shaft, "So, both of you have come to dismantle my evilness, which I'm so proud of. You will die if you keep going forward. As you see, there is a wooden door in your sight. Beyond the door, you will find all the answers to your questions."

The Dublin Trio and Thor huddled. They agreed to separate as Thor went forward in the mine shaft, and the Dublin Trio would cross the door's threshold to see what lay beyond. It wasn't long before the Trio was beyond the door that he started to hear his mom's voice in his head from when he was a little boy. He remembers an incident when he did something wrong and his mom chastised him. Hearing his mom's voice in his head really shook him, but he knew it was Satan who was behind it.

He cleared his head, regained focus, and said to Satan, "If that's all you got, then you're in big trouble."

"I hate all of God's creation, especially humanity. Who are you to defy me?" replied Satan. "You'd better bow down before me before I destroy you."

"I live by many principles, and here's one of them," said the Dublin Trio. "Cowards die many deaths before their death, but the hero tastes death but once. Guess who the coward is? I'm not bowing down to a coward like you, with all your scare tactics. Don't expect me to be afraid of you, for I believe in God's inexhaustible power."

Satan stopped engaging, the Dublin Trio navigated himself out of the hallway, and found an exit where he found Thor. Both men saw the room from which the evil resonance was coming. Then, six of Satan's evil lieutenants appeared, from the back of the room, ready for battle. As the six lieutenants came closer, the Dublin Trio and Thor readied their positions for battle. The Trio saw hard hats on a rack from the coal mine's past and threw one to Thor to protect his head. The Trio also saw a shovel, which he also threw to Thor, who was well-versed in many fighting styles.

The Trio picked up a pickaxe and removed it because it was cumbersome. He could use a good piece of lumber with his martial arts skills. This battle was street fighting elevated to an art form. No wasted motion, every blow meant to inflict maximum damage, every dodge meant to create an opening. They weren't just swinging; they were feinting, weaving, using their momentum, and exploiting weaknesses. The pick barrels, blunt as they were, became extensions of their will, delivering punishing, concussive blows. They rolled with punches, twisted out of grabs, and countered with a flurry of strikes, knees, and headbutts – the infamous "Dublin Kisses."

Thor, a leviathan of quiet destruction, faced the other three lieutenants. His shovel, a humble tool, became a weapon of shocking versatility. He used its wide blade to parry the razor-sharp talons of one, the long handle to trip another mid-lunge. When the third tried to circle him, Thor whirled, bringing the flat of the shovel around in a devastating arc that sent the lieutenant sprawling, a wheezing sound escaping its shadowy form. He wasn't relying on fancy moves, but on relentless, unyielding force, every swing powered by a lifetime of hard labor and an iron will. He ducked under a swipe, then plunged the shovel's point into the ground, levering himself up and over a charging enemy, landing behind it to deliver a powerful, two-handed blow with the shovel's edge across its spine.

The fight was a cacophony of grunts, impacts, and the alien shrieks of the lieutenants. Sweat gleamed on the faces of the Dublin Trio and Thor. They took hits, absorbed impacts that would shatter lesser men, but they never stopped moving, never stopped fighting. Their breathing was ragged, their muscles screamed, but their eyes blazed with a fierce, unwavering resolve.

The Dublin Trio and Thor stood panting, surrounded by the dissipating remnants of their foes. Their bodies ached, blood trickled from cuts, but their eyes held the clear, steady light of victory. They had prevailed, not just through brute strength, but through their raw guile, their streetwise instincts, and the unbreakable bond that formed their courage. It was a testament that truth always will prevail, born not from fear, but from a fierce will to protect, always overcomes any ambition, no matter how grand, that is born from fear. The evil resonance still pulsed, but it was vulnerable. The Dublin Trio and Thor were ready to dismantle it. At that moment, Satan manifested himself and stood before the evil resonator device and said, "You think your abilities are superior to mine?"

The Dublin Trio responded, "The truth is the truth, and that will always come to the surface. You represent evil, and your time is running out."

"Your biggest enemy is time," added Thor. "Because our outcomes always have a high degree of honor."

"My source of energy comes from an inexhaustible level of energy that is beyond your comprehension," said Satan.

"What is the source of your energy, and where does it come from?" The Dublin Trio countered. "It comes from an empty well where you keep chasing your tail only to find emptiness."

"We just kicked your top six evil lieutenants' asses, and you're next," said Thor. "Either you get out of our way, or we'll run you over".

"We believe in a God infused mind, and we feel this is so much more superior than you in so many ways," said the Dublin Trio.

"Your power is insignificant compared to the power of positive thinking and compared to will and tenacity," said Thor. "And to think that you thought you were superior to man for 10,000 years, I laugh at you,"

Satan shouted, "Enough! You will die for those remarks." Satan then unleashed a wave of energy so intense that it brought Thor and the Dublin Trio to their knees. Still, they refused to give in, despite reeling in pain. The Dublin Trio recalled being surrounded by coal. Coal is an energy conduit that can augment energy. The Dublin Trio quickly gathered his wits to plan his next move.

Thor saw this and said, "When we're right, we fight; we have to pull ourselves together and get up." They slowly rose, much to the astonishment of Satan. The Dublin Trio then said, "Supreme God, I have learned through my travels that you like to imbue your universal jewels in your glory, and I ask you, on behalf of your Mother Earth, to use the coal in this mine shaft to engage Satan for your glory and for us to prevail."

Soon after, the Dublin Trio saw that a beam of white particles came and descended on the mine shaft, engaging the coal and augmenting its natural power. This energy surrounded Satan in a whirling pattern, which he disliked intensely. This natural power, blessed by God, defused the evil energy resonance from the mine shaft. Satan quickly exited the scene. The Dublin and Thor know from their heart that the power of believing is the ultimate power. They felt good as they exited the mine shaft. They felt blessed, having witnessed God's limitless creative power and experienced the grace of God upon them for a job well done.

The lesson from this story is that the dark side is associated with our lower personality traits, like the ego. For instance, ego can be related to aggression, bitterness, jealousy, and judgmental behavior. It is our lifelong journey to confront these weaknesses with prayer and self-evaluation. When we do that, we can become better people, as we go into our golden years before we meet our maker.

Professor Catherine Gozalez

A theology professor named Catherine Gonzalez, who was in her 90s, speculated that Jesus and Mary Magdalene may have been married. She placed the pieces together, but was too old to do the legwork to follow them where they led. Therefore, she went online to see if she could get help to finish her research. She came across the Dublin Trio, a man of faith and courage who served three tours as a Green Beret special OPS officer, and she thought he was the best man to finish the job.

The Dublin Trio was at the local Kung Fu martial arts studio, brushing up on new techniques. Upon returning home, he discovered a request on his website to assist a professor of theology in completing her research on the possibility that Jesus and Mary Magdalene were married. Still, she's too old and senility is starting to set in, so she wants the Dublin Trio to drive out to see her at her home in Nazareth, PA, about a two-hour drive from Philadelphia.

When the Dublin Trio arrived, Professor Catherine Gonzalez explained that she had spent several years piecing together evidence that Jesus and Mary Magdalene may have been married. Still, at the age of 92, senility was starting to creep in. She didn't have time to finish her research and wanted the Dublin Trio to complete the work for her. She laid out the framework of her research. There was enough evidence to construct a narrative that explores this possibility, drawing on various interpretations and alternative perspectives. She explained to the Dublin Trio that one key element was the expectation of Jewish men at the time Jesus was living in Israel that marriage and procreation were highly valued and often considered a religious duty.

The argument was that it would be unusual for a prominent figure like Jesus to remain unmarried. So, Professor Gonzalez gave the Dublin Trio two years' worth of notes, files, and her research findings. The Dublin Trio took them to a theology historian and asked him to put everything in chronological order. This theology historian was into black magic and did not want this inspirational story to go public, so he went into his black magic spell book, and found a spell that he could cast that would lace the verbiage of the notes and the research paper with dark energy that when absorbed by the reader it would have a devastating effect.

The Dublin Trio returns home, starts organizing and reading the content. He realized he wasn't feeling good from reading the evil energy-laced content, so he went to his bedroom to try to recover, but the uneasiness only increased until his abdominal area felt like he ate poison. So, he crawled out of bed and put his head on the floor and simply said, "God Help Me." Suddenly, he felt a bolt of divine energy hit the top of his head, it circulated down to his abdominal area, cleansing the evilness from his body. The divine energy rested in the abdominal area, engaging and cleansing until the evil energy was gone. The Dublin Trio rose to his feet and went to his bakers' rack, where he had a collection of religious items to pay tribute to God, and thanked God profusely for his divine intervention. Over the next several days, he went to work digging up the supporting evidence that Jesus and Mary Magdalene were married.

Mary Magdalene played a highly significant role among Jesus' followers. The gospels mention her numerous times, more than most other apostles. She is present at crucial events like the crucifixion and resurrection, being the first of two witnesses to the risen Jesus. The Gospel of Philip depicts Mary Magdalene as Jesus's closest disciple, potentially his companion, suggesting a special relationship. While mainstream Christianity does not consider the Gospel of Philip canonical, it offers a different perspective on her role.

The Gospel of Mary Magdalene, which was excluded from the New Testament canon, emphasizes inner spiritual transformation and the presence of God within each individual. It also portrays Mary Magdalene as a key disciple who receives special teachings from Jesus, particularly after the resurrection. It highlights her role in revealing these teachings to the other disciples. The gospel also challenges traditional views on authority and leadership within the early church, suggesting a more inclusive and spiritually based approach. Her Gospel presents a path to spiritual knowledge and liberation that is not dependent on external rituals and doctrines, but rather on an inward journey and understanding of the true self. In this gospel, Mary Magdalene emphasizes Jesus' post-resurrection revelations as he imparts them to her. The focus is on themes of overcoming fear, understanding the nature of sin, and the importance of inner peace. The gospel of Mary elevates Mary Magdalene's role as a leader and teacher, particularly in contrast to Peter, who initially questioned her authority.

This notion that Jesus and Mary Magdalene were married had spread to the highest authorities over the next two thousand years, and it was safeguarded by the likes of Chinese Empress Wu Zetian (624 AD), who was the only Chinese empress and had significant achievements marked her reign. She opened up the government service to a broader range of people, including commoners, based on merit rather than birth or wealth. William Wallace, of Scotland, knew of this. He was a Scottish knight and national hero who played a key role in the wars of Scottish Independence. Lastly, there was King Henry VIII, who was king of England from 1509 until he died in 1547, and he was aware of this. He established the Knights of the Garter, who were dedicated to the king for all his causes. All these figures were sworn to secrecy of the notion that Jesus and Mary Magdalene were married.

The Dublin Trio also suggested that Jesus may have introduced a new religion during the Last Supper, specifically through the Eucharist, also known as Communion, which represents a new covenant. The bread and wine of the Last Supper are a symbolic representation of Jesus's body and blood, given for the forgiveness of sins. Jesus established a new covenant with his followers, replacing the old

17

covenant given through Moses. Therefore, the Dublin Trio concluded that Jesus set out to break away from Jewish tradition to forge a new religion, which put the wheels in motion for Christianity to evolve, which now inspires 2.4 billion people around the world. More importantly, events after the Last Supper set in motion a momentum that spread through the Roman Empire. Ten percent of the Roman population were Christians after the death of Jesus, and it grew to 60 percent by 350 AD.

This grassroots effort snowballed, affecting Roman authority and ultimately leading to the collapse of the Roman Empire from within. You have to realize that the Roman authority was in place for 2,200 years. The Dublin Trio pondered that the most significant superior force on Earth came to an end from a loving, inspired, peaceful religion called Christianity, and it only goes to show you that the power of love is the most extraordinary power in the world.

The Convicts for a Higher Cause

The Dublin Trio is on a passenger train carrying two dangerous convicts who are being transported to USP Lompoc in California. While the guards were taking the convicts down the aisle and placing them in their seats, which required cuffing and re-cuffing them, both convicts overcame the guards and took a hostage. They made their way to the front of the train, where they tied up the engineers and took control of the train. The Dublin Trio was aware of the situation and was thinking of ways to get to the front of the locomotive. In the meantime, the two convicts start talking with each other and the hostage, a woman. One of the convicts asks, "What are we going to do once we're free from this situation?"

The woman hostage, a Lutheran pastor, says, "You can take Jesus's advice when he was at the well with the Samaritan woman and drink from a well that will never go dry, and it will always give you eternal life." One of the convicts says," What did Jesus ever do for me?"

"As with anything, it all starts with a ripple in the pond," said the pastor. "A ripple in your consciousness, when you start to believe, then your salvation will start. God never gives up on anyone, including you. Thousands and thousands of people have had a change of heart once they have shown that first interest in God and continued down the enlightened path."

As the convicts consider the pastor's words, the Dublin Trio is assembling the pieces to reach the front of the train as quickly as possible, to assist in any way they can. In the meantime, the woman pastor continues to educate the two convicts.

"I don't know what both of you did in your past, but faith is about reflection and redemption," she said. "You have to realize that faith is stronger than any past transgression that you may have had. No power in the universe is stronger or comparable to God's faith. Because once you go down the enlightened path, you start to realize that the intangibles of faith, like being patient, being focused, having the highest clarity of mind, being joyful, loving life."

She continued, "Living a contentful life is your daily armament against the pitfalls and negativity of life, but it all starts with you. Once you make the first investment, the door of knowledge is open to you, and all you have to do is walk through it. It doesn't happen overnight, but everything in life is a process, and this is a wisdom that is eternal."

The two convicts listened, the one more than the other, and the one who was half-listening said, "Do you know what I don't like, when we're doing road crew and picking up trash all day along the highway and after a long day of picking up trash, the prison officer watching over us says to me, 'You forgot a piece of trash.' I really hate that. I spent all day picking up trash, and he's going to pick out one piece that I missed. Well, he can kiss my grits."

The other convict, who was listening more earnestly to the pastor's message, said, "Do you know what you're going to do? You're going to pick up that piece of trash and do your job to the best of your ability. Then you're going to go back to your cell and put your weary head on your pillow and realize that if you can be humble, do the smallest details, and take pride in your work, then you can become a CEO in any company."

As this was going on, the Dublin Trio was finalizing how to get to the front of the locomotive to assist, in whatever way possible, to bring the runaway train with all the passengers on it to a stop. He noticed a circus troop on the train, equipped with all their gear. He approached the ringmaster and asked if it was possible to use the cannon. He sought expert advice from the person who shoots himself out of it, known as the Human Cannonball. The Dublin Trio wanted to be shot out of the cannon and catapulted to the front of the train. The Trio wants the Human Cannonball to show him how to somersault through the air and break his fall as he lands. He plans to use the football safety gear that one of the clowns in the circus uses to help break his fall.

So, the Trio, the circus ringmaster, and the Human Cannonball pulled the cannon onto a flatbed, which is connected to the passenger car, and the Dublin Trio went into the cannon and lit the end of it. Before you know it, he was ejected from the cannon and flying through the air. As he was in flight, he tucked his head downward so that he would land in a manner that was the least harmful to him. As he descended, he pulled out his carabiner, knowing he would have to latch onto something. The problem is that he overshot the train, and as he descended in front of it, he tried to break his fall but couldn't latch onto anything. He felt that he had no choice, because he thought that the momentum was too much. The next thing he knew, he was down below the front of the locomotive. He still had his carabiner out, which he latched onto his belt. Finding something on the train to connect it, he was suspended in front of the locomotive by the carabiner in his belt.

This gave him a chance to catch his breath and get his senses together. Once he did that, he was able to reach out with his hands to the front of the train and hoist himself up, regain some balance, and pull himself to the entrance on the side. He entered the train to find the two convicts and the hostage. His first question was if the woman was alright. The two convicts, not in the mood for surprises, picked up a metal pipe when he arrived. At that point, the Dublin Trio said, "I am unarmed and I pose no threat to you. I was wondering if I could give any assistance with this train, which is traveling way too fast on these tracks. So, whatever your goals are, we'll never get there with the lethal speed this train is traveling."

As the Dublin Trio was saying that, a helicopter was following the train from above. The Dublin Trio said to both of them, "I think both of you should give yourselves up to the authorities and ask for mercy.

This is your best strategy because when it's sincere, people love a redemption story, and you can tell the warden that you had a lot of time to think about your life while being up here in the locomotive cabin."

"I counsel a lot of people in my profession, and if you surrender now, I can vouch that I counseled you," said the pastor. "I can say that I feel that both of you were regretful of your actions. I wouldn't say that if it wasn't true. You could do your time and learn about the wonders of God's Kingdom, and when you get out, a whole new life is waiting for you."

With that said, the two convicts slowed down the train to a stop and surrendered to the authorities. As the oldest adage in the universe states: When one door closes, another one will open.

The Dublin Trio Confronts the Aliens

A clairvoyant person who lived in the area noticed something was vibrationally wrong in the atmosphere. He had been studying this transition for several weeks and saw that people were acting strangely. He remembered Dublin Trio's name from an article in the paper when the Trio returned from his tour of duty with the Green Berets. So, this person found the Dublin Trio and explained his case to them.

The Trio listened to him with sincerity because he had a lot of credentials as a clairvoyant. The Dublin Trio researched how to detect energy vibrations and discovered information about a dowsing rod. This device is a forked branch typically held with each hand grasping one of the forks, acting as a receiver for vibrations or subtle energies from the surrounding area. Some believe that the stronger the movement of the rod, the closer or more abundant the hidden resource.

So, the Dublin Trio went into the woods with his trusted dog to find the ideal dowsing rod, and they found it. After seeing the dowsing rod, the Dublin Trio, being a man of God and all his Kingdom, said a prayer so that he may have the nature spirits' blessings.

"Creator of all life, I come before with the nature of your beauty, your majesty reigns supreme through all your creations, including the nature spirits," said the Dublin Trio. "There's something wrong in our community, and only through your guidance and intervention with me, in your splendor of artistry of nature, I ask your blessings on my endeavor to uplift your holy name. In the name of all the Holy Ones that walked the Earth to glorify you. Amen"

The Dublin Trio suddenly felt the dowsing rod come alive with vibration, and this gave him guidance over the next several days. The Trio ventured deeper into the woods until he stumbled upon, to his shock, an alien spaceship hidden within. Unbeknownst to the Dublin Trio, the aliens in the spacecraft had captured three people before he arrived. The Dublin Trio thought the safest thing to do was to observe the spaceship from a distance. He felt that the alien spaceship was here for malicious purposes. With his dog by his side, the Trio kneeled and told his dog to stay put. Then Dublin Trio pulled out his crucifix, looked at it, pondered, and realized that anything can be accomplished through risks and sacrifice.

He then started to stroll towards the alien spaceship, while saying the 23rd Psalm, *"The Lord is my shepherd, I shall not want. He makes me lie down in green pastures. He leads me beside the still waters. He restoreth my soul. He leads me in the paths of righteousness for his name's sake. Yea, though I walk through the valley of death, I will fear no evil, for you are with me. Your Rod and your staff, they comfort me. You prepare a table before me in the presence of my enemies, you anoint my head with oil. My cup runs over. Surely goodness and mercy shall follow me. All the days of my life, and I shall dwell in the house of the lord forever."*

As the Trio approached the alien spaceship, a ramp descended, as if to invite the Trio to enter. The Dublin Trio took a deep breath, walked up the ramp and into the alien spaceship. He was greeted by three aliens who looked human but had a few distinct differences. They asked the Dublin Trio to sit down and wanted to know how they had found the spaceship. The Dublin Trio explained how the dowsing rod worked and the aliens were intrigued with the Trio's ingenuity and decided to study him further. The aliens informed the Dublin Trio that the gender balance between men and women on their planet is not equal. They have a large proportion of men on their planet, and they came here to study human behavior. As they study humans, the factories on their planet are producing large cargo ships to transport women to Earth, where they are forced to assimilate into the culture and marry men to further their society.

"We have been watching the human race for some time now," said one alien. "We feel your hunger to evolve over the centuries from a primitive race to a race of knowledge and exploration. We believe that if you continue to evolve at this pace, you will potentially match our technological capabilities, driven by your pursuit of knowledge. We are hopeful that the assimilation of your women will coalesce with our culture, and we will be even more superior than any other species in the universe."

"Let me ask you a question," said the Dublin Trio. "On Earth, here, the gender mix, from what I understand, is pretty good, pretty equal. There are reasons for everything. Earth is a profoundly spiritual planet, and many believe that a higher power governs global events. This higher power watches over us and governs us as a population. Do you worship a God on your planet?

"No! We worship no one and feel that we are in control of our own destiny," replied a second alien.

"But you are not in control of your own destiny because you have to come to Earth to bring cargo back to your planet," countered the Dublin Trio. "Namely, woman from earth, for your own self-serving needs."

"Shut up! We don't accept lectures from an inferior race," said the second alien.

"Yet, your gender mix is off and ours is not," said The Dublin Trio. "We worship a higher power, and you don't. If you're so superior, why can't you figure out the right solution to your problem? Everything in the universe is a creation of God, and when you worship God, you get reciprocal benefits. Your planet has a gender mix problem, and our planet does not. What is the difference? Our planet generally believes in a God, and we feel that God takes care of us."

The Dublin Trio continued, "Your solution to your problem is very labor-intensive, if you consider all that you are doing to solve your problem. God's love and intervention are an expression of gratitude. And there is no commerce involved, just pure thankfulness."

The aliens paused, then a third one said, "You say that God is the creator of the universe and all living things. How do you suppose we start worshiping this God that created the universe?"

"Everything starts with prayer," said the Dublin Trio. "Prayer is a petition to God for change from past action and asking for a new path forward with his blessings and guidance. Would you like to join me in prayer on your behalf for your planet?"

The aliens consider their situation and the extra costs they are willing to endure to solve their problems. It then occurs to them that they can fix all their problems with prayer. So, they allow the Dublin Trio to proceed on their behalf with a prayer.

The Dublin Trio said these words: "Supreme majesty of loving God, I would like to humbly come before you today on behalf of the alien race that is visiting Earth at this point and time. They are joining me in prayer for your guidance and intervention in their society and culture, seeking the highest divine good and outcome. They are asking you for redemption, so they can move forward with your love and help them rebuild their humanity with your blessings as they start a relationship with you. From all the holy ones that walked the Earth, Amen."

The aliens felt a very subtle grace come upon them that they had never felt before, and they now know of this Higher Supreme God that the Dublin Trio was talking about.

"I recommend that you spread the word out to your community about the power of prayer and worshiping

God, your creator, for the highest good," said the Dublin Trio. The aliens released the people they had captured, allowing them to leave in peace for a better tomorrow.

The Tree Lady

There was a lady who lived in a hut in Tacony Park, Philadelphia, and was psychic. She understood that trees could communicate with each other through various methods and networks, including above-ground signals. She did her psychic readings from inside the hollow of a large tree. The locals called her the "Tree Lady" because she was very intuitive and gifted. One day, a young man named Harrison came to see her. She conducted a reading for him, utilizing her intuition to explore his past, present, and future.

By using tools, like crystals and runes, she gained an extraordinary perception of this young man. She gathered he was destined for something much larger down the road. She wondered why this young man was chosen for a life of blessings and trials, given that people with his skills usually attract darker forces.

She was worried about him and said to him, "You have an extraordinary gift. One day, you will realize your own potential, but listen to me, someone of your ability will attract attention from the forces of evil, and they will try to control you. You must not give in and always pray to God for your salvation, for he is your strength and protection. Good luck, and you can always count on me if you need me." The young man in question went on his way, continuing his path to enlightenment.

Seven years have passed, and now the man is 25 years old, has a good job, and has met a wonderful woman named Terry. Unknown to him was that this woman sought him out because she practiced the dark arts and Satan had access to her. She understood that her job was to demoralize him and destroy him mentally. They went about having a relationship, which seemed great and was very mutually beneficial. As the relationship progressed, she started to become cruel to him by playing mind games with him and leaving him bewildered and distraught.

One day, while walking back to her apartment during a thunderstorm, a lightning bolt suddenly flashed down, striking Harrison and knocking him to the ground. Terry watched in delight because evil ran through her. She knew that Harrison was a man of nobility and of great potential, so she watched with glee as smoke emitted from him after such a lethal strike. Then, to her shock and surprise, Harrison started to pull himself together and move his arms around. Terry quickly shifted gears and began to act concerned. Soon, Harrison was on his feet again, and Terry wondered, "What kind of man is this, who can endure a lightning bolt and still live?" Harrison wondered the same thing, but he felt different, as if a low electrical current was running through his body. He remembered the Tree Lady and wanted to go back to her for more answers.

He goes back to Tacony Park and finds the Tree Lady. When he saw her, he reminded her of who he was. The Tree Lady remembered who he was because she thought about him from time to time. Harrison explained to the Tree Lady what happened to him when he was hit by lightning, hoping she could offer some insight. She said the body is made up of spiritual voltage and spiritual current. The human body comprises a naturally conductive system that reacts to electrical and energetic currents.

"You had a gift, meaning your spiritual voltage system was already advanced," said the Tree Lady. "So, when the lightning bolt hit you, you were well prepared to absorb it."

This gave Harrison much to think about on his way home. He thought about how the universe works in relation to humanity, which made him think of it like an orchestra. The intertwinement of God's collective universe, which aids the human race from God's Kingdom to God's Divine Cosmos, is evident in the nature spirits and the work of His hands, which is all around us. As he pondered this, he came across a natural freshwater creek. He was worn out from all that had happened, so he took the path down to the creek.

He put both hands into the creek and said, "Loving God, may the purities and divine nutrients of this freshwater creek filter through my body, rejuvenating me in your glory. Not my will, but your Divine Will. Amen." He then felt a purity of cleansing energy that entered his body, which felt so good that it lifted his spirits, and he left the creek a new man.

Harrison felt exhilarated as he left the creek and wanted to buy Terry flowers from a local supermarket on the way home. He picked up a bouquet of lilies and joined the line to purchase the flowers. While waiting in line, he realized there was nectar in lilies. He took a deep breath, feeling the nectar integrate with his lungs. It felt as though the nectar was being distributed throughout his body, purifying it. Terry was happy to see him as he gave her the flowers.

They talked, and she seemed more interested in him than she had been previously. They decided to walk across the street to a coffee shop. Soon, a car ran the red light, came around the corner, and struck Harrison, knocking him to the ground. Terry knelt over him, waving and beckoning for people to help him. She looked down at him with concern, as tears came down her face, while she was jostling Harrison to come to life. Terry's heart began to transform from a cold-hearted state of hate to one filled with love. Harrison's eyes opened slowly. Some passersby helped Harrison to his feet and helped him back to Terry's apartment.

Once there, Terry said to him, "Are you okay, Harrison?"

"I'm fine, how are you?" Harrison asked.

"Harrison, you saved me in many ways," said Terry, and then they embraced.

The Truth Will Always Prevail

The Dublin Trio decided to go camping one weekend at the Bear Creek Camping Grounds, about a one-hour drive from Philadelphia. After the Dublin Trio put up a tent at the campsite, he took a walk at night. It happened to be a beautiful night with the stars shining, so the Trio decided to take a quick break and absorb the beauty of the stars. As he was watching, he noticed, to his amazement, that one star was moving closer to him. As it moved closer to him, it shrank in size to avoid revealing its enormous size.

When it finally reached the Dublin Trio, it stopped about 20 feet before him, and it was about the size of a basketball. Then it spoke to him. "I am the North Star, the most powerful and respected star in the Milky Way. I am considered the symbol of hope and love in the universe. I have a message for you from God. God says you're doing a good job, but you'll need help with your next mission. In the Blue Ridge Mountains of Pennsylvania, a secret tunnel from the past remains. It was used for coal mining. There is a powerful wizard who has become proficient with

Satan's power, and Satan's resonance runs through him. He is an expert in martial arts.

Twice a year, evil worshipers of Satan come and access this hollow area through the tunnel, and they worship Satan. Your job is to confront the wizard and show him what true power is. We aim to empower you with the natural elements: fire, trees, the ocean, and the celestial star galaxy. These elements will strengthen you for your mission. Pray to God before connecting with each element. Good luck, and Godspeed."

After saying these words, the North Star vanished, and the Dublin Trio stood in awe, for he was giving a message from the Most High. *Much work needs to be done for this mission,* the Dublin Trio thought. Unbeknownst to the Dublin Trio, Satan has contacted the wizard through vibrations that God has chosen someone to destroy his evil infrastructure hidden in the Blue Ridge Mountains. The wizard had Dublin Trio's name and, bolstered by evil's energy, felt cocky enough to look up the Dublin Trio's phone number and call him to try to rattle him.

The Dublin Trio was home going about his business, preparing for his next mission and the phone rang. The Trio answered it, and the next thing he knew, someone was on the other end shouting expletives and threats at him. The Dublin Trio, being shrewd in diverse communications, decided to let whoever this was exhaust their rant before he responded. The other person's message summarized that he was going to kill and make a mockery of the Dublin Trio in front of all his evil worshipers.

"You must be the punk that conducts worship services for Satan," said the Dublin Trio. "I'm going to kick your ass and teach you a lesson about real power."

The wizard says back to him. "We'll see." That was the end of the phone call. Yet, the wizard was worried, since the Dublin Trio was so forceful in his comeback.

In the meantime, the Trio had to follow the North Star's guidance to strengthen themselves. He headed to Ocean City, New Jersey, and booked a room near the beach for the night. He woke up early the next morning, around 6:00 AM, to catch the sunrise over the Atlantic Ocean. The Dublin Trio waded into the ocean to about chest-high water and enjoyed cresting the waves, hoping this was what the North Star had in mind. Suddenly, he felt the ocean's nutrients entering his body. It felt so pure, with a hint of saltiness and a touch of energy. As this was happening, a school of dolphins went before him. It was the most fantastic thing he had ever witnessed, and he wondered if this was a message to solidify what he was feeling.

The Trio came out of the ocean renewed with vigor and was ready for his following item on his quest of fulfilling the elemental requirements by the North Star, so he booked a star gazing night cruise in Ocean City for that night. It was going to be a clear night, so the Dublin Trio entered the yacht and joined the rest of the passengers. As the yacht ventured into the darkness, the stars became much clearer. The Trio made his way to the back of the boat, where there were no passengers. He looked up into the sky and instinctively raised his palms to face the galaxy of stars. He said, "Supreme God, please let the energy of your divine stars descend on me."

To the Dublin Trio's amazement, he saw the body of stars glow with energy, coalescing together, and then flow down to the Dublin Trio. The energy entered his palms, and he felt the celestial body enter his body, fortifying him with its power. He felt revived and more vigorous. Now, he must think about his next task, which is the power of trees. Before the Dublin Trio began his next task, he wanted to learn more about the power of trees. He knew that trees are good for our well-being by improving our physical and mental well-being. They act as natural filters, absorbing pollutants and releasing oxygen.

The Dublin Trio visited Neshaminy State Park in Bucks County, Pennsylvania, a place known for its many trees. He found a path down to the embankment by the Delaware River and saw an old, wise tree that was still robust in nature. The Trio looked up at it and said this affirmation on behalf of the tree: "Living Tree with your roots so grounded that they help you bring strength and might to your outstretched limbs of hope that bring us your renewal each spring, your essence of believing is instilled with your contribution to humanity. Holy God, please allow the nurturing and greatness of this tree to coordinate with my body's chemistry for the highest divine good." Then, suddenly, he felt a profound connection to the natural world around him, as if he were one with it, which gave him powerful feelings of centeredness and serenity, akin to the strength of an oak tree.

Once the Dublin Trio arrived home, he was anxious to confront the wizard in the Blue Ridge Mountains, but he had to complete one more task given to him by

North Star. So, he built a large fire in his fire pit in his backyard, and once the fire reached a roaring stage, the Trio said the following prayer: "Loving God, please allow your fire spirit of transformation and purification to clear away the old and make way for the new. For all new beginnings start with you, and please allow this fire to be a transformative power, invoking motivation and igniting an inner strength for growth." The Dublin Trio experienced increased energy and vitality, akin to being powered by a steam engine, accompanied by a tingling sensation, a slight feeling of heat, and subtle, purifying burning sensations.

Now, with the four natural elements inside the Dublin Trio, he feels much more vibrant and stronger, and ready to take on his mission. So, the Trio, filled with nature's bounty, set out for the Blue Ridge Mountains near Carlisle, Pennsylvania, where a tunnel from the early 1900s, used for coal mining, exists. He found his way to the tunnel and proceeded inside into the worship grounds where the wizard performs his honoring of Satan's demonic ways. The Dublin Trio works his way around the facility and enters the wizard's private room, a side room beside the main worship room for the evil congregation. The Dublin Trio sees the wizard preparing for his lecture for the evil doers, and the wizard notices him.

"Honestly, who's rummaging through my sacred scrolls now?" The wizard muttered, his voice a low growl. He spun, his movements fluid, belying his age.

The curtain parted just enough for a figure to slip through, silent as a shadow. "Surprise, Professor," said The Dublin Trio, who appeared as a lean silhouette against the dimly lit passage as he stepped into the room. His hands were already up, fists loosely clenched, eyes sharp. "Ready for a Kung Fu lesson?"

The wizard smirked, a predatory glint in his eye. "Ah, the Dublin Trio. I had a feeling my lecture would attract some... 'unwanted' attention." He shifted his weight, his stance widening. "Here to stop my enlightenment, are we?"

"Your enlightenment, or your campaign of utter malarkey?" the Trio shot back, a hint of disdain in his tone. "Either way, it ends tonight."

"Then let's dance, my friend," the wizard purred, lunging forward. His first strike, a lightning-fast palm heel, whistled past the Trio's ear. *WHISH*. The Trio ducked, a quick *whoosh* of air, then countered with a blur of his own. A rapid-fire flurry of blows, each aimed at pressure points. *THWACK! THUD!* The wizard parried, his forearms deflecting the strikes with surprising force.

"Not bad, for a common meddler!" the wizard grunted, a short, sharp laugh escaping his lips. "But I've faced worse!"

Their battle was a whirlwind of motion, a silent, deadly ballet. They moved through the antechamber, knocking over stacks of ancient texts, sending quills scattering. A crystal orb cracked as the wizard slammed the Trio against a pedestal. The Trio rebounded, a fierce kick aimed at the wizard's midsection. The wizard staggered, but his eyes never left his opponent.

Suddenly, the wizard saw an opening and lunged. He sent the Trio flying backward, through the velvet curtain, and into the grand hall. A collective gasp rose from the assembled congregation of cloaked figures. "

"What in the blazes?!" One cultist shrieked.

"Oh, my stars!" A woman gasped.

The fight exploded onto the main stage, under the glow of eerie green lights. The audience, a sea of bewildered faces, recoiled. The wizard, fueled by the public spectacle, moved with renewed ferocity.

"Witness, my loyal followers, how I crush the insolent!" He bellowed, with a triumphant grin spreading across his face.

The Trio met him blow for blow, the sounds of their impacts echoing through the vast chamber. *CRUNCH! WHUMP!* The wizard, despite his age, moved with incredible agility, his martial arts mastery evident in every block and strike. The Trio, equally skilled, tested the wizard's defenses, searching for a weakness. Their struggle led them to the center of the stage, where a grotesque, suspended apparatus hung from the ceiling. It was a sacrificial platform, adorned with dark runes. With a sudden burst of speed, the Dublin Trio leaped. *WHOOSH!* He grabbed onto the platform with both hands, his body swinging like a pendulum.

"What in the—?" the wizard said, looking up, his eyes widening. With a powerful surge, the Trio swung his body forward, both legs shooting out like pistons. *THWACK!* A devastating two-legged kick slammed into the wizard's chest. The wizard cried out, a strangled "Urgh!" escaping his lips, his breath knocked clean out of him. He stumbled backward, collapsing to one knee, clutching his chest.

"No... not like this..." he wheezed, struggling to rise. Before the wizard could even push himself up, the Dublin Trio was on him. A blur of motion, a final, decisive strike. *WHAM!* A powerful sidewinder kick connected with the wizard's head. The wizard's body went limp, collapsing onto the stage with a dull thud. A stunned silence fell over the congregation. Not a hum, not a moan, not a single laugh broke the quiet.

The Dublin Trio stood over the defeated wizard, his chest heaving, and the Dublin Trio turned towards the worshipers and said, "And this is your leader, this is your hero? I am here by the empowerment of God and God's Angelic Kingdom with the nature spirits. We want to carve out a new path for you that will help you spread your wings beyond your limits, where God's immense power exists for each individual. There is power in individuality, as long as you seek a unified power that is eternal and will never give up on you."

Then, slowly, the wizard came to his feet while the Trio was speaking, pulled a switchblade, and attempted to stab the Trio from behind. One of his women supporters saw this, and was on the stage with him, ran and jumped on his back before he stabbed the Dublin Trio. The Trio turned, easily disarmed him and put his foot on the wizard's throat. At that moment, the wizard had a change of heart, and the Trio saw a slight change in the wizard's eyes that indicated awareness. The Trio lifted off his foot, backed up, and the grace of God descended on the wizard in fine white particles. The wizard knew he was in the midst of a power he had never felt before.

The Dublin Trio turned to the congregation and said, "This is what God is all about, judgment and redemption, because he is the ultimate redeemer. God will never give up on you, and you are always welcome in God's house. I challenge all of you to walk a new path, and this path will lead you to a well that will give you eternal power."

The worshipers exited the mountain through the tunnel as the sun rose, signaling a new day for all people to regenerate, renew their faith, and glorify their God through their actions, for all things are possible when one has hope.

The Wise Lighthouse Keeper

There was a 175-year-old lighthouse off Cape Cod in Massachusetts. Since the 1950s, a great-grandfather has been the keeper of this lighthouse. He let his grandkids run up to the top of the old lighthouse because they were curious. When they got to the top and looked out, they saw something peculiar: a Russian fishing boat that was hunting whales. This was illegal, banned, and largely prohibited by the International Whaling Commission. They ran back and told their great-grandfather, and he couldn't believe it. So, he took a look for himself. Despite having weak legs and a bad back, he climbed the steps and saw the Russian fishing ship hunting whales off the coast of Cape Cod.

The old lighthouse keeper didn't want to call the Coast Guard because he didn't want any noisy questions about his felony conviction when he was a careless teenager. So, he found the Dublin Trio to investigate the situation. Unknown to everyone, the Russian ship has been off the coast of Cape Cod for several days, waiting for orders from the Kremlin to proceed. So, the Dublin Trio brought his sleeping bag to sleep at the top of the lighthouse to monitor the situation 24 hours a day. On the first night, he happened to be looking out onto the coast, and to his astonishment, he observed an SOS signal coming from the Russian ship. So, the Dublin Trio thought to himself, why is the Russian ship sending an SOS signal from the boat? He felt this needed more investigation.

When morning came around, he took his binoculars and looked upon the ship's deck, but he didn't see anyone in distress. So, the Dublin Trio went to the closest marina and rented a motorboat, so he could get close enough to the Russian ship to learn more. During the next night, he took the motorboat, positioned it near the Russian boat, set anchor, and then swam to it, pulling himself up on one of the ropes alongside the ship. Once on board, he maneuvered like a panther in the night. Being a black belt in Kung Fu, he moved down the decks with stealth to learn why the Russian ship was there. Finally, he overheard two sailors talking about their plan, which was to detonate a nuclear bomb that was on the boat.

They were discussing their fate, aware that they were on a mission with a high risk of failure on behalf of their government. Still, they also knew that this would be a lethal blow to America's biggest city, namely New York City. The Dublin Trio realizes that the whale hunting is probably a smoke screen, so it had to be stopped. Not known to the Dublin Trio, the captain of this ship lost his wife in a tragic accident many years ago, and several days ago, he answered a mayday call from a yacht with a father and daughter on board. Once the father and daughter were on the ship, the captain could not help but notice a striking resemblance between the father's daughter and his deceased wife when she was younger. This led to clouded judgment on the captain's part. He had the father sequestered on the ship and insisted that the daughter join him on the bridge because he wanted her presence, as she reminded him of his dead wife. The more the yacht owner's daughter was in the captain's presence, the more delusional he became in this situation. He even handcuffed her to the chair, insisted that she join him at the officer's dinner table, and expected her to wear one of his wife's gowns that he had with him. The captain became increasingly delusional about the yacht owner's daughter.

After the Dublin Trio overheard the two sailors, another sailor approached him and asked him if, by any chance, he had received any of the SOS signals sent from him the other night. As the two men continued their conversation, the man who sent the SOS signal confided in the Dublin Trio that, in his heart, he couldn't knowingly cause the infliction of horror and pain that they were ordered to carry out. This intrigued The Dublin Trio. As two sailors continued their conversation, the man who sent the SOS signal told the Trio that on board was a nuclear bomb, which he already knew about.

The man who sent the SOS signal was a man of peace and wanted to assist the Dublin Trio. So, the Dublin Trio asked this man where the nuclear bomb was located. The man led the Dublin Trio to where the nuclear bomb is, so the Trio can attempt to disarm it. The two men went deep into the vessel, and the Dublin Trio followed this man of peace until they found the nuclear bomb chamber. Two heavily armed men guarded it. Despite this, the Dublin Trio had to get access to that room.

The salt spray stung The Dublin Trio's face as he picked up a piece of timber, its rough edges digging into his palm. The Russian freighter groaned beneath his feet, the metal leviathan cutting through the churning gray sea. New York was only hours away from oblivion if he failed. He tightened his grip, the 2x4 feeling reassuringly solid. The chamber door loomed ahead, flanked by two hulking figures in drab green uniforms. Their AK-47s hung loosely, but their eyes were sharp, scanning the corridor. "Halt! State your business," barked the taller of the two, his voice thick with an accent the Trio recognized from his time in Chechnya. He smirked, hefting the timber. "Just admiring the architecture."

The other guard chuckled, a guttural sound, and said, "You're a long way from the tourist deck, friend."

"Is that so?" The Trio feigned surprise. "I must have taken a wrong turn. Tell you what, why don't you point me in the right direction?"

"We have orders," the first guard said, his hand now resting on his weapon. "No one passes without authorization."

"Orders are meant to be broken," The Trio replied, his voice hardening. He shifted his weight, the timber now held ready. "Especially stupid ones."

The first guard sneered. "You think you can take us both?"

"I know I can," the Trio said.

He moved in a blur of motion, before they could react. The timber whistled through the air, connecting with the first guard's temple with a sickening thud. The man crumpled, his rifle clattering on the steel deck. The second guard roared, swinging his AK-47 around.

The Trio ducked under the barrel, the cold steel grazing his hair. He slammed the timber into the guard's midsection, doubling him over. The guard gasped, trying to regain his breath. The Trio didn't give him the chance. He spun, using the momentum to bring the timber crashing down on the back of the guard's neck. The man went down hard, his body twitching. The Trio stood over them, breathing heavily. He tossed the timber aside, the sound echoing in the narrow corridor. He knelt, checking their pulses. Unconscious, but alive. Good, he thought. He wasn't a killer, just a deterrent.

He reached for the access panel beside the chamber door, his fingers flying over the keypad. A green light flashed, and the heavy steel door hissed open. He stepped inside, the cold air of the chamber washing over him. The nuclear device sat in the center of the room, a gleaming metal cylinder humming with deadly power. He took a deep breath, steeling his nerves; it was time to get to work. He glanced back at the timber lying discarded in the corridor. A wry smile tugged at his lips. "You can never go wrong with nature's best friend," he said to himself. With urgency at hand, the Dublin Trio went to work to deactivate the nuclear bomb. He had difficulty because he wasn't familiar with the wiring on this particular bomb. He noticed the bomb had a regimented time sequence for when the bomb goes off the coast of New York City. The Trio had to seek out his ally, the peacemaker on the vessel. He found him and asked him to use his Morse code light signals to contact the great-grandfather, who was a lighthouse keeper. Soon, the Trio was sending SOS signals off the boat, hoping the lighthouse keeper, a World War II veteran, might recognize them. The SOS signals started to unfurl from the Trio off the ship, and sure enough, the lighthouse keeper knew what to do.

In the meantime, the captain's delusional mind deepened as he continued to have the yacht owner's daughter appear in his dead wife's gowns. After dinner, the captain would have the daughter entertain him by dancing with him in the ballroom of the captain's quarters. Word got back to the Dublin Trio that this was happening in the captain's quarters. The former lighthouse keeper, in the meantime, called the Coast Guard about the situation with the Russian ship, and they said they were going to intercept it.

As the Coast Guard was sending a ship out to stop the Russian vessel, the Trio went to the ship's engineering room and was determined to sabotage the ship's propulsion system so the Coast Guard could find them more easily. First, he worked to disengage the cylinder conduits to ensure they couldn't sail at maximum speed. He then rerouted power to provide the vessel with auxiliary power, thereby avoiding suspicion that something was wrong with it.

The Coast Guard showed up with swift force, with helicopters and high-speed intercepting boats demanding that officers from the Coast Guard board the vessel. The Russian vessel's captain had no choice but to stop the ship and be boarded by the Coast Guard. Once the Coast Guard boarded the boat, the

Dublin Trio grabbed the yacht owner's daughter and handed her over to the authorities for safekeeping. The Trio alerted the officers of the Coast Guard that there was a nuclear bomb on board the vessel, and they called in their explosive disposal specialist team to deactivate the bomb. In the meantime, the captain of the ship escaped to his private motorized raft.

The Dublin Trio saw this happening, and he climbed the railing on the vessel and dived headfirst into the turbulent waters and climbed on board the raft where the captain was located. The captain put the raft on autopilot, and Dublin Trio and the captain engaged in a fist fight with a lot of wrestling and jockeying for position, as the raft aimlessly went forward. The captain got a clean fist shot on the Trio, which knocked him out of the raft, but the Coast Guard was in pursuit, and they threw a rope line onto the captain's boat.

So, when the Dublin Trio fell out, he was able to grab onto the rope line and pull himself back to the captain's raft. He snuck up on the captain from behind, grabbed him by the neck, and pulled him back to the seat. The Trio then grabbed the rope and lassoed it around his neck. Next, he took his carabiner, hooked it to the seat, and used more rope to tie himself up. The Coast Guard apprehended the captain, and the crew was arrested for espionage and violent crimes against the United States. Back at the ship, the Dublin Trio informed the captain of the Coast Guard unit of their military credentials, and the captain gave the Trio a well-deserved salute for a job well done.

The Pranic Healer

There was this married couple who lived in Warrington, Pennsylvania, a suburb of Philadelphia, and they had two children. The couple's names were Marianne and Sean. Something peculiar happened each time someone sat in the family's recliner. When someone sat in the recliner, they felt a sense of irritability and agitation. This had been going on for about three months. About two months prior, while Marianne was in the kitchen, Satan approached her.

She heard him talk, but couldn't see him. This vocalization was terrifying. Satan told her that he wanted her to do his bidding in the physical realm to facilitate his evil. Satan threatened to kill her unless she complied, so she reluctantly agreed to his terms. Then, instructed by Satan, she obtained a red brick and put evil markings on it. This gave the brick power from Satan. She placed the brick under the recliner so that when anyone sat in the recliner, they would feel an evil presence.

In addition to the brick she put under the recliner, Satan instructed her to place three additional evil red bricks positioned outside the house, in the flower beds.

These extra bricks would radiate a malevolent energy that would negatively affect the well-being of other family members in the house. He also instructed her to burn candles throughout the home at a specific time to glorify him. Marianne asked Satan why he was doing this, and Satan said, "Your husband has become a very gifted, proficient pranic healer, and I intend to stop him."

In the meantime, her husband Sean continued his pranic healing practice from his healing room, which he had in his house. He worked with clients who had a wide range of ailments. A pranic healer is taught to access prana energy, which is the universal sea of energy that infuses and vitalizes all matter. This sea of energy makes up the building blocks of all matter that manifests in the physical world. Prana is also the power that flows in all living things and performs all vital functions.

The prana is facilitated by concentrating on accessing this universal energy, and a trained pranic healer will facilitate this through their hands and onto the patient. The goal is to replace old stagnant energies with fresh revitalizing prana. This fresh energy will reinvigorate a person's chakras to ensure they operate at a high capacity, facilitating healing. One of the tools that pranic healers use is the chakra system. Chakras energize the body's major vital organs. They are like power stations that supply prana to the body's major vital organs.

When the power stations malfunction, the vital organs become sick or diseased because they lack the prana needed to function. Through this practice, a healer's hands become highly sensitive to various forms of energy. So, Sean's decided that something had to be done with the recliner. He examined it and found a red brick at the bottom of the recliner. Sean removed the red brick, took it outside, and placed it on the deck railing to examine it. He knew that fresh running creek water would neutralize the evil energy, so he took the brick to a nearby creek and threw it into the water with a prayer.

One night, Sean and Nancy were watching television together, laughing and having a good time. Sean sees a dark cloud emerge from beneath the wall and crawls along the floor. To his astonishment, it entered Marianne, making her skin pale. The next thing he noticed was that his wife transformed into an old hag, only to slowly revert to a younger woman, but not the same person. Sean was convinced the dark cloud came from an evil source. So, the next day, when no one was home, Sean, who was fed up with the evil presence in his house, went upstairs to the master bedroom and said, "Satan, you're not so bad. I'm here, right here. I dare you to come into existence in front of me so that I can kick your ass!" Sean then tore off his shirt to demonstrate his seriousness and waited, but Satan never manifested.

Sean committed himself to saving his wife. So, one night, while Marianne was sleeping, Sean tried to perform pranic healing on Marianne to help remove the evil in her life. This went on for several nights, and then one morning, Marianne looked dejected and said to Sean, "Please stop performing pranic healing on me, I can't be saved."

Sean felt bad for his wife, but he wasn't going to give up. Then, one day, Sean was walking through a nearby state park, and he started to think about how everything in God's universe is interconnected and how all of God's blessings are fueled for a purpose. He once read that consciousness is related to nature spirits, such as plants, rocks, rivers, earth, fire, the sun, and air. Sean starts thinking that he must pray to God for the angels and the might of the nature spirits to come to his wife's aid and help cleanse her and protect her. Just as when he was ready to pray, Satan appeared and he talked to Sean, "I am the beast that came into being to crush and destroy the human spirit. You might know me as Satan."

"You took my wife away from me, and I plan to get her back, you son of a bitch!" Sean replied. "And now with this prayer, you will see the true power of God's majesty, for there is no power greater than the power of love."

Sean then said these words: "Supreme Loving Almighty God, source of all life and goodness, this prayer is offered for my wife, Marianne. I request your cleansing grace to descend on her to remove any evil spirits as described in your scriptures and to bring healing back to her pure heart. Your protective presence is asked to surround her, safeguarding her in body, mind, and soul, echoing this sentiment of Psalm 91, verses one and two, which speaks of dwelling in the shadow of the Almighty. Also, invited are your holy angels from the glorious kingdom to be Marianne's guardians and guides, shielding her from any harm and negative evil influences. Furthermore, I am praying that Marianne finds solace and strength in the natural world that was created. May the beauty of creation in the whispering wind and gentle rain remind her of the constant presence of love and bring her peace and renewal, for this is where God's regenerative power works. Amen."

Suddenly, Satan felt the mighty rise of the natural world around him, and he didn't like it. He got out of Dodge fast, and Sean went home. From a distance, his wife looked normal. When Marianne saw him, she ran and leaped into his arms for a loving embrace. Despite the odds, a new day of hope is worth pursuing when you believe.

The Missing Children

In a town called Townfair, located in Bradford County, Pennsylvania, they have been dealing with an issue for some time now, and it has reached a critical stage. The citizens want to get a resolution before it gains national attention. Three children, aged nine to twelve, were missing. People in town wanted to bring in a real pro to help the local authorities, so they found the Dublin Trio online. He seemed perfect for the job and was located a four-hour drive from Townfair.

After the Trio finished cutting his lawn, he went inside his house to check his messages and heard an urgent message from the folks in Townfair, asking for his help. In the message, they provided a synopsis of the issue, which was alarming to the Dublin Trio. The Dublin Trio made arrangements to travel to Townfair and was on his way, with all his gear, the next day.

Once he arrived, the Dublin Trio wanted to get to business immediately and interview the parents whose children had disappeared. After interviewing the three parents, one of the parents brought to his attention that one of the children may have fallen into a bottomless cavern in the hills near Townfair. He thinks the Dublin Trio should check it out. The Dublin Trio spoke to another parent, who mentioned that he was a hunter.

Recently, he had gone into the woods near the town and saw large insect footprints leading to a large cavern. The other parent leaped and suggested that when the nearby missile silo was deactivated, something might have gone wrong, allowing radioactive waste to contaminate the soil, which could have enlarged some of the insects. This was news to the Dublin Trio regarding the former missile silo. He asked about their whereabouts so that he could look into it. That night, the Trio used his security clearance to access information about the missile silo, and all the paperwork looked good. Still, he ordered a chemical protective suit from Amazon, which he would wear the next day when he visited the silo. The next day, the Dublin Trio visited the missile silo's location to assess its activity and discovered the hatch.

He broke the chain that locked it, opened the hatch to the silo, climbed down the ladder, and saw that the missile was still intact. To his shock, he realized that it was leaking radioactive gases from nuclear reactors, and it could spread through the atmosphere. This was horrifying to the Dublin Trio, because it was negligence to the highest degree. After all, the submitted paperwork indicated that all nuclear materials had been removed; however, someone failed to do their job and submitted the documents as if the work was complete. The next consideration is that the insects may have substantially increased in size due to the radioactive leakage. This is where his deduction is going, as hard as it is to believe. Still, three children are missing. The Dublin Trio is starting to get a bad feeling about this. The next thing to do is explore the caverns, which the Trio does the next day.

The Dublin Trio enters the cavern and rappels down to the surface, following the large insect's footprints, and he proceeds down the cavern tunnels. Suddenly, an enormous centipede crawls around the corner and heads towards the Dublin Trio. The Trio sought cover under a large rock until the centipede was over him. He took out his rope and lassoed the exterior sternite of the centipede's underbelly and pulled himself up. Once he was under its belly, the Trio took his hunting knife and fatally stabbed the centipede. He sensed that the centipede was going to collapse, so the Trio jumped to the ground and leaped out of the way as the centipede collapsed. Lots of thoughts entered Trio's mind after an encounter like this. Did the radioactive leakage have something to do with the enormous size of that centipede? Are the enlarged insects behind the missing children?

The Dublin Trio continues down the cavern corridor, and as he walked about fifty feet, something significant was unearthing itself from beneath the soil in front of him. It continued to grow in size in front of the Trio, becoming a large spider that was at least 25 feet high. The spider reached out and picked up the Dublin Trio with the end of his legs. As the spider lifted the Trio, he picked up a five-foot stick from the ground. As he was about to be devoured by the spider, he took the stick and poked the spider's eye, causing it pain, which made the spider release the Trio. He hit the ground hard, but was not hurt. He continued down the corridor with the spider in pursuit. The Trio ran down the path and came across a break in the path. It was an immense, deep gorge that he couldn't see the bottom of. Then the Trio took out his rope, lassoed it around a branch above the gorge, and swung across the deep gorge, landing on the other side. He arrived just in time to set a trap for the spider.

The Dublin Trio planted a log across the gorge that reached the other side. He hoped to entice the spider to cross the gorge using the log. Sure enough, the spider arrived only to analyze the situation. So, the Trio started to provoke the spider to cross the gorge by yelling, "Come on, I'm right here, come and get me!" The spider crossed the canyon, and when it reached the middle of the log, the Trio kicked the log so that it would fall with the spider into the gorge. The Dublin Trio then lassoed his way across the gorge and went looking for the children. He proceeded down the cavern tunnel and found another tunnel that intersected with the central tunnel. He went down that tunnel and found a large room.

To his shock, he saw the three children entangled in a large web spun by the spider. He rushed over to untangle them, freeing all of them from the web. By this time, the townsfolk had heard of the Dublin Trio's presence and why he was in their town. A large gathering of people was outside the cavern, since they heard that he was inside the cavern. The Dublin Trio emerged from the cavern with the three children, and the townsfolk were overjoyed to see the children and have this issue resolved. The Dublin Trio reported the radiation leak to the Environmental Protection Agency for clean-up. The Dublin Trio continued his quest, given by God, to help out people who may have lost hope.

The Golden Fleece

There was a 12-year-old boy who was playing in his backyard in the Lawndale section of Philadelphia. As he was playing, his leg went through a hollow area of the backyard. It looked as if his leg had disappeared into the grass turf, and this surprised the boy. He was inquisitive about how this happened, so he got his father to come out and help him investigate the situation. The boy's father got out a shovel from their basement to unearth the grass where it was hollow. What was revealed was a larger cavity around the area where the boy's leg went through the turf, and this was very perplexing.

As the father and son are looking into the cavity, they see a red brick path going deep into the earth. They are both curious as to why this is in their backyard. So, the father goes into the basement, retrieves a ladder, puts the ladder into the cavity, and goes down the hole with his flashlight. Once at the bottom of this vast hole, he could see what looked like an ancient passageway. He thought he should bring in a professional to explore the passageway, but not the local authorities, because he did not want to cause a panic. He searched the Internet for someone with a specialty in this particular situation and found the Dublin Trio's services.

The Dublin Trio arrives the next day, goes down the ladder with his flashlight, and starts to explore the ancient passageway. As he's going down the passageway, he comes across a tree. He noticed something unusual on the tree and reached out to touch it. It was the softest material with a note that said, "I am William Wallace and this is The Golden Fleece. To whoever finds this Golden Fleece, you have been entrusted with a significant responsibility, for this Golden Fleece has the power to influence land disputes and outcomes beyond your imagination. Good luck!"

The Dublin Trio took the Golden Fleece from the branch, returned to the surface, and shared it with the father, along with the note from William Wallace. Wallace was a Scottish Knight from the 13th century. The Dublin Trio asked the father if he wouldn't mind trying to do some good in the world with the Golden Fleece. The father gave the Dublin Trio permission to use the Golden Fleece temporarily.

The Dublin Trio went home to research the Golden Fleece, aiming to find out what historical records are available on this relic. Based on what historical records are available about this item, the Trio learned that the Golden Fleece was made of ram's wool, specifically a ram with golden wool, sired by the sea god Poseidon. The gods sent it to rescue Phrixus. After Phrixus reached the land of Colchis, he gave the fleece to King Aeetes, who kept it in a sacred grove.

The Dublin Trio thought that the Golden Fleece somehow ended up in William Wallace's hands, and he saw firsthand how the Golden Fleece can influence the outcomes of land disputes and tilt the balance of power with its abilities. The Dublin Trio began to consider how he could harness the power of the Golden Fleece to bring peace and stability to a place on earth that desperately needed it.

The Dublin Trio first thought of the land dispute between China and Taiwan. The conflict between China and Taiwan revolves around Taiwan's political status, with Beijing asserting its One China principle over Taiwan, and Taiwan maintaining its independent, democratic government. This disagreement has deep historical roots and continues to fuel military, political, and economic tensions.

The Dublin Trio believes he has much to learn before understanding the powers of the Golden Fleece, so he continues his research to gain a deeper knowledge of its purpose and abilities. In particular, Jason, from Jason and the Argonauts, was sent on an impossible mission to prove he deserved the crown. By completing the impossible journey to the far-off land of Colchis and returning with the fleece, the myth reveals that its actual power was not enhanced magic; instead, its power was to instigate a hero's epic journey. As a magnificent and nearly unattainable prize, the fleece serves as a catalyst that forces Jason to become a hero. Without such an objective, Jason might have remained a man of unresolved potential.

The Trio pulls out a map of Asia that shows China and Taiwan, holds the fleece and says, "I surrender my needs to God, the Kingdom, and with the universe, which understands all my needs and my goal of helping to protect Taiwan, in the event of an invasion." and he places the fleece over the map.

The Dublin Trio soon realizes there is great power within the Golden Fleece and goes to the local pharmacy to pick up some medicine to clear his head. While he was waiting in line, he noticed a woman observing him. So, he got out of line, walked up to the woman, and asked her, "Why are you looking at me"?

She said, "You are a man on many questions."

The Dublin Trio was intrigued with what she said, because she was right that he had a lot on his mind, and she went on to say, "I have the answers to your questions. The universe always provides the answers when you are ready to listen. I'm a psychic who works a few doors down the street, and I advise you to come in for a session."

So, the Dublin Trio went to the psychic's place of business, sat down with the psychic, and she said, "You have the opportunity within your grasp to give guidance to the suppressed, and the universe has heard you. I have the answers you need. Unbeknownst to Taiwan, China has 35 missile launchers hidden and aimed at Taiwan in the event China launches an invasion. This is the reading that I'm feeling the need to pass on to you."

"Taiwan would need to know that so they could knock them out with a surgical strike, if they thought an invasion was imminent, said Dublin Trio. He gathered the information from the psychic and felt he should relay this information about the missile launchers in

China to his former Green Beret commander, who has ties with the Pentagon. People at the Pentagon would know what to do with this information.

There are many valuable takeaways in this story. Still, I would like to emphasize to the reader that the universe is compelling and willing to assist in meeting your needs. You need to pray to God and share your needs with Him. Ask him to include the Kingdom and the universe in facilitating your needs. Always remember that there is often a result behind action, prayer, and manifestation.

Dublin Trio and Doctor Dolittle's Grandson

A travesty occurred in the deep woods of Rwanda when someone known for her groundbreaking research and intense efforts to save mountain gorillas was murdered in December 1985. Her name was Dian Fossey, and her research focused on ethology and primate behavior. The authorities who investigated her murder found a ransacked cabin, with signs of a struggle, a hole cut into the wall, and her body found near her bed.

While poachers were suspected due to her activism, evidence suggests a more sophisticated, planned act, potentially connecting her to her research and enemies she made in her conservation community. Sadly, the murder case remains unsolved, and the Rwandan government looked high and low for the right person to conduct an independent analysis of the murder investigation. They decided to reach out to the Dublin Trio to share some new insights on the murder investigation.

The Dublin Trio lands in Rwanda and gets to work. He studies the evidence and feels that the poachers were behind her murder for many reasons. The Dublin Trio feels that the poachers and their collaborators were threatened by her anti-poaching methods, which involved physically destroying traps, confronting poachers, and providing support to park guards. Poachers were responsible for hunting and killing gorillas, either directly or by setting traps.

Dian Fossey directly confronted them and worked to stop their activities. The Dublin Trio began to wonder if he could communicate with the gorillas, as they might have some valuable information. He learned in college that gorillas possess innate instincts and acquire learned behaviors through social learning, which are then passed down through generations. But this isn't what he specializes in. So, he began educating himself on how to communicate with the gorillas. He learned that Doctor John Dolittle, a British medical doctor from the 1800s who became a veterinarian after discovering he could communicate with animals, has a grandson who can also communicate with animals and lives in Rusiz, Africa.

Where Doctor Dolittle's grandson lived wasn't far from Rwanda, and the word is that he retired there. The Dublin Trio decided to go there to see if he could help him with the investigation. The grandson lives in a cabin with no phone service, and since his cell phone is not publicly known, the Trio had to hike to his cabin. As he walked through a section of the path lined with foliage on both sides, he heard a rustle of something significant above the jungle noises. He looked up, and that's when he saw it: A monstrous anaconda, easily 25 feet in length, slithering through the branches. Its scales gleamed with the slickness of the jungle's embrace. The Trio's heart hammered in his chest as he realized the creature was headed straight for him. In a split second, the serpent's body unfurled, and it dropped like a silent, deadly rainbow, landing heavily on his shoulders.

The impact was stunning. The anaconda's thick coils began to tighten around his neck, cutting off his airflow. Panic surged through him, but the Dublin Trio knew that struggling would only make things worse. With a desperate gasp, he managed to draw in one last breath before the pressure grew unbearable. He felt the world begin to darken at the edges, his thoughts growing hazy. Yet, the survivalist within him was stubborn, unwilling to let go without a fight. With trembling hands, he reached for the hunting knife sheathed at his side, the weight of it comforting in his grasp.

The blade was cold and sharp, a reassuring presence against the suffocating warmth of the anaconda's body. His vision swam, but he remained focused. His thumb found the serrated edge and slid it along the snake's throat, feeling for the right spot. The anaconda reacted violently, trying to coil tighter, but the Dublin Trio's arms remained firm, his grip on the knife unyielding. He could feel the creature's pulse, a rapid throb against his fingertips, and knew he had to act fast.

With a surge of adrenaline-fueled strength, he plunged the knife into the soft flesh of the snake's throat. The anaconda writhed in pain, its coils loosening slightly. The Trio took advantage of the moment, slicing deeper, his movements precise and swift. The snake's movements grew weaker, and he felt the pressure on his neck start to ease. Then the

Dublin Trio removed the anaconda from his neck and sat on a nearby log to regain his strength for the remainder of the trail. Once fully rested, the Trio resumed his journey to see Dr. Dolittle's grandson. The Dublin Trio pitched a tent for the night and woke up the next morning as the sun came up over the mountains. He was inspired, for a new day had dawned, and the Trio gathered up his gear and continued down his trail. It wasn't too long before he found Doctor Doolittle's grandson, whose name was Gary. Gary retired from the work that had been passed down from his grandfather. Still, he had heard of the senseless murder of Dian Fossey and was willing to help in any way he could.

They hiked back to the Dublin Trio's cabin, where they went over the available clues from the murder investigation. Gary wasn't sure if the silverback gorillas would communicate with him, but it was worth a shot. The next morning, the Dublin Trio and Gary went out to the area where Dian was known to communicate with the silverback gorillas. They were hoping to get close enough to the gorilla family so Gary could find a way to connect with them. Gary walks out into the open a little bit, starts mimicking and sounding like something that he learned from his grandfather. This sound was indistinguishable to human ears; the Dublin Trio stood there intrigued. Gary kept making this sound, and he had faith in this sound that was audible, although it had no clarity to the human ear. To the surprise of the Dublin Trio, he started to hear the rustling of the brush beyond the clearing, and something was coming their way. It wasn't too long before several silverback gorillas came out of the brush and into the open.

Gary approached them cautiously with his palms out. Then, Gary went into a language that was inaudible to human ears. The gorillas rose, appearing as though they were actually listening to what Gary was saying. One gorilla walked approximately four feet forward from its clan. The gorilla looked as if it was trying to communicate with Gary, and Gary was listening. When the gorilla was done, Gary approached it calmly with his palms out, and this gorilla was receptive.

They embraced for a brief moment in solidarity, and the gorilla rose and went back into the brush. Gary was moved to tears by what the silverback gorilla told him. As he composed himself, he went into the Trio's cabin to discuss the situation, for any meeting of the minds between man and animal is a transformative occasion. Gary explained to the Dublin Trio what occurred. The silverback gorilla reported that the poachers left Dian Fossey's cabin, got into their vehicles, and headed to their hometown of Kagitumba, Uganda, located north of Rwanda.

With this new information, which came 40 years after the incident, the Dublin Trio is hopeful the Rwanda authorities can pick up the trail in Kagitumba, Uganda. And who knows? Anything is possible when you don't give up the cause. Nature has its own set of rules and laws, and when you combine nature with believing with hope, anything is possible.

The Cellar Basement Door

The Dublin Trio was raised on a tree-lined street in a neighborhood in Philadelphia called Oakwood. In this neighborhood, his parents lived in a 16-foot twin home, which was built in the 1940s. He moved into this house when he was about 8 years old. As he grew, he started to develop a kind of clairvoyance that included honing in on hunches and vibes in certain situations. Ever since he moved into this house, a young Ryan would get creeped out by the old, weathered wooden door in the back of the house, under the porch. He was unaware at the time that his hunches and vibes were beginning to develop, but he had a strong sense that something was off beyond that door.

One night at the dinner table, when he was 12 years old, Ryan's parents spoke of a handyman they had used about four years earlier, who had worked on the walls underneath the porch in the area that Ryan perceives as creepy. Little did Ryan and his family know that the handyman who worked on the walls was into animal sacrifices, worshiped Satan, and planted a python snake skull in the wall for safekeeping. The information about the handyman did not diminish young Ryan's hunches and vibes about what was beyond the door.

Nevertheless, Ryan has grown up and is now 18 years old. He has passed all the requirements to join the elite Green Beret Special Ops Unit. There is one thing he wants to do before he joins the military, and that is to confront his fear and walk beyond that wooden door in the basement. So, he goes downstairs and opens the wooden door underneath the porch, walks in, stands in the middle of the room, and tries to let his senses go. He feels the creepiness, and it's getting worse. Something more sinister, but he's not sure. Ryan leaves the room, but is aware of his feelings and gets ready for his assignment with the Green Berets.

After 12 years and a decorated career in the Green Berets, Ryan Shamus returns to Philadelphia only to find out that the city condemned his childhood home, because it started to sink due to an underground creek beneath his house. Still, he wanted to get back to his house to explore the room beneath his porch again. So, Ryan returned to his childhood home and snuck in through the front porch window. He made his way down to the basement, where the cellar door was located. Upon entering, he realized that something had been dug out from the left-hand wall. It was very noticeable that something had been removed. Ryan was trying to put all the pieces together in his head. The hunches, the vibes, the creepiness, and now the wall that had something removed. He then noticed that the window to the basement cellar room was open, allowing someone to access the room. Ryan was perplexed about what was happening and decided to reach out to a childhood friend. This friend, a private detective, would help him figure out the situation. Ryan managed to get fingerprints from the window and give them to his friend.

The friend, a private detective, arrived within a few hours and observed the scene. Both of them could see that something had been dug out of the wall. The friend took fingerprints from the window and sent them off to get analyzed. Once the results came back, they had the name of the man who came in through the window.

The next day, Ryan visited the man's mansion in the woods to gather information about his intentions for the old house. When he got there, no one was home. So, Ryan looks through a window, and, to his surprise, he sees the skull of a large snake, possibly a python, on a table in the living room. This skull looked like it was just recently unearthed, given the mud covering it. Ryan thought that this might have been taken from the wall underneath his porch. As crazy as it seemed, Ryan had to consider all possibilities at this point. Still, Ryan had to gather more evidence. So, he went around the back of the mansion and noticed that the back door was open. He entered the house from the back door and went to the room where the snake's skull was to examine it.

Upon examining the snake skull, he discovered a small voodoo doll inside. There was a name on the voodoo doll, and that name was Pastor Finigan Murray. He was a renowned spiritual preacher, and many people throughout the globe looked up to him for inspiration.

We're starting to put the pieces together and realize that the owner of this skull had evil intentions. He stored the skull in the room under my porch in the wall for safekeeping until he was ready to come back for it. Ryan thought.

Close to the skull, there was an advertising booklet with an ad on the back of it. The ad featured the mansion's address, surrounded by a circle. It listed a seance that was scheduled for tonight, and it said, *Prince of Darkness Séance.* All details about the séance were in the ad, and there was a handwritten message that said, *Call Marcus.* Ryan believes the snake's skull will be a part of the séance tonight. He had seen enough and thought it was time to call in three other former Green Beret officers to break up this party tonight.

As the sun dipped below the horizon, casting long shadows over the abandoned mansion, Ryan felt a familiar rush of adrenaline. He had returned to the lair of darkness, a place where his past and present collided. The air was thick with anticipation; tonight, an evil séance was set to unfold, orchestrated by a notorious figure from his past, Marcus, and his band of malevolent worshipers.

Ryan wasn't alone. He had called upon his former Green Beret comrades: Jake, Sam, and Leo. They were each a master of hand-to-hand combat, and each had a heart that beat for justice. They approached the mansion with stealth, their years of training guiding their every step. The moonlight glinted off their determined faces as they exchanged silent nods, ready to confront the darkness that awaited them.

Inside, the atmosphere was charged with a sinister energy. Candles flickered, casting eerie shadows on the walls as Marcus and his followers chanted in a language lost to time. The air crackled with malevolence, but Ryan and his team were undeterred. They burst through the door, a whirlwind of righteous fury.

"Enough!" Ryan shouted, his voice cutting through the chant like a knife. The worshipers froze, their eyes wide with shock as the four warriors stepped into the dim light, a force of nature against the encroaching darkness.

"What do you want?" Marcus sneered, his confidence unshaken. "You think you can stop us?"

With a swift motion, Jake lunged forward, taking down one of the worshipers before he could react. Sam and Leo followed suit, engaging the others in a flurry of fists and skillful maneuvers. The once confident worshipers found themselves outmatched, their dark intentions crumbling under the weight of righteous valor.

Ryan faced Marcus, their eyes locking in a battle of wills. "This ends tonight." Ryan declared, stepping closer. The tension was palpable as the two men circled each other, memories of their shared past igniting a fire within Ryan.

With a sudden burst of speed, Marcus lunged, but Ryan was ready. He sidestepped, delivering a powerful counterattack that sent Marcus sprawling to the ground. The remaining worshipers, witnessing their leader's defeat, faltered, their resolve wavering.

One by one, the Green Berets dispatched the remaining worshipers, each blow a lesson in morality and strength. As the last of the dark figures fell, the room fell silent, the oppressive energy dissipating like mist in the morning sun.

Ryan stood over Marcus, who was now gasping for breath, a look of disbelief etched on his face.

"You thought you could summon evil without consequence?" Ryan asked, his voice steady. "Tonight, you've learned that true strength lies in righteousness."

With that, the four Green Berets left the mansion, the echoes of their victory resonating in their hearts. The evil worshipers had received their attitude adjustment, a reminder that light would always prevail over darkness. As they walked into the night, Ryan felt a sense of peace wash over him, knowing they had made the world a little safer, one battle at a time.

The Ancestors of Robin Hood

The ancestors of Robin Hood currently live in Pennsylvania and are having a family reunion. They decided to honor their family heritage by taking up the cause of redistributing wealth from the rich to the poor. Still, they sought someone sympathetic to their cause who could help facilitate such a noble gesture. Someone at the reunion heard of the Dublin Trio's noble acts and suggested him.

He was contacted by the family, which led to a meeting between the Dublin Trio and some of the ancestors of Robin Hood. They began discussing how to facilitate their cause in today's world. The Dublin Trio emphasized that they wouldn't participate in anything involving robbing a bank or taking money from a legally operating business. So, they continued to talk, and someone from Robin Hood's family suggested that maybe we could break up a drug exchange, and they could intercede and take the money. Sometimes those exchanges can result in a substantial amount of money, which the family can then give to those in need.

The Dublin Trio thought about what he said and, after going through his deduction process on this suggestion, thought it was a worthy idea. So, the Dublin Trio and the ancestors of Robin Hood started to formulate a plan on how they were going to do this. It would require someone of the Dublin Trio's talents and cunning street smarts to go into the underworld, poke around, and see what kind of information he can come up with. The objective was to get information on a drug exchange, and the Dublin Trio and Robin Hood's ancestors would be staked out there as well. (They are experts in archery, just as Robin Hood was.) The objective is to intervene in the drug trade to seize this cash and distribute it to the poor.

So, the Dublin Trio starts snooping around, asking some questions, and he finds out that a gang leader may have some answers to some of his questions. He goes through the appropriate channels to meet with the gang leader. When he sits down with the gang leader, the Dublin Trio is honest with him about his intentions. Although this gang leader has had a life of speed bumps with the law, there was still a noble side to him. He wanted to help the Dublin Trio. Therefore, he told the Trio about this man who keeps his ears to the pavement, who is wise beyond his years, and knows the goings on of things.

"If you know what I mean," said the gang leader in reference to this person. "If you take care of him, he may help you with what you want. He likes to do his business at 19th and Cambria Street in Philadelphia. He's easy to spot because he's always wearing a jeff."

They wrap up the meeting with the gang leader asking some questions about what missions the Dublin Trio did as a Green Beret, and the Dublin Trio said, "They are classified, but trust me, I've seen it all." The gang leader got up, gave him a fist bump, and the Dublin Trio was off to the corner of 19th and Cambria.

The Dublin Trio saw the man wearing the jacket, and they spoke. The Trio explained to the man what his purpose was and slipped him a $100 bill. The man in the jeep told the Trio there was a vacant lot in the Portmount neighborhood where the boxcars meet up on the outskirts of Philadelphia. A massive drug deal coming out of Central America will go down, and the exchange is happening on Monday at midnight.

The Dublin Trio and Robin Hood's ancestors prepare for this exchange between the drug cartels and the buyers, both of which are heavily armed. This requires a lot of focus, which led members of the Hood family to fine-tune their bows, as they plan to be well hidden behind the boxcars on the railroad tracks during the exchange. The Dublin Trio is in deep meditation to gain more focus for this encounter. The Dublin Trio plans to pack a hunting knife and a 9-millimeter gun for this mission.

It is now Monday night, and it's close to 12:00 AM, and the archers from the Hood family are in place behind the boxcars. Dublin Trio is also hidden, waiting for this exchange to take place. They wait and wait, and a few minutes after 12:00 AM, several cars pull up into the vacant lot, and the Dublin Trio and the Hood family are in position. People get out of their vehicles, and they're in plain sight. One guy in the group gets the urge to have a cigarette. He separates himself from the rest of the group and enjoys his cigarette. The Dublin Trio brings himself to the attention of the man having a cigarette. The smoker saw the Dublin Trio. The Trio had to act quickly without making a stir or a lot of noise in this situation.

The Dublin Trio took out his hunting knife, assessed the problem, and threw it, and it sailed through the cold air. End over end, looking for its target, and after piercing the air for 40 feet, it landed squarely into the smoker's chest, and he collapsed. But it wouldn't be long before the rest of the group would be looking for him. So, the Dublin Trio gave the signal to the Hood family archers to act when everybody was out of their cars. The Hood family archers released their righteous arrows, which landed swiftly and precisely on target. After the exchange, all the money was packed into a duffel bag.

The Dublin Trio moved in, picked up the duffel bag, and then he and the Hood family members took off with the money. When they arrived at the Hood's house, they counted the money and realized there was about $1,000,000 in the duffel bag. They were pleased that the funds would be used to help the poor and the needy.

Spiritual practice of tithing is critical. The energy behind tithing is rooted in the spiritual principle of giving and receiving, which is believed to align one's heart and finances with a divine flow of abundance. Rather than a mere financial transaction, tithing is viewed as a discipline that produces internal, energetic shifts.

Nature's Bounty

The Dublin Trio took a walk in a park in Chalfont, Pennsylvania, and came to a clearing. Out of the woods came a baby red panda, native to the area, who approached the tip of his shoe and looked up at him, as if to say, "Please help me find my mother."

The Dublin Trio, feeling concerned for the cub, picked it up and went into the brush looking for its mother, but couldn't find her. He then Googled on his phone what kind of sound a red panda makes and learned it makes a low-pitched sound. The Dublin Trio had a dog whistle, which makes a low-pitched sound, and they used it. To his amazement, the mother red panda came out of the hollow log that was nearby. When he saw this, he put down the red panda cub, and it ran to its mother. Dublin Trio felt at peace with himself for how often does one get to contribute to reuniting a panda cub with its mother?

The Dublin Trio continued to walk alongside a natural creek, and to his astonishment, he saw a blue heron swoop down onto the creek, grab a fish, and fly back up into the air again. Blue herons have been in existence in North America for about 1.8 million years.

The Trio continued to follow this path alongside the creek deep in the forest. He kept going until he came to an incline, and he climbed this incline to the top. Once at the top, he saw a huge valley where you could see for miles, and it had a huge pond. It was breathtaking, and he marveled at the beauty of the valley's scenery. In the center of the valley, he saw a woman. The Trio did not want to disturb her, nor did he want her to feel uncomfortable with his presence. So, he sat at the very top of the hill to show that he was no threat to her. The woman saw him and waved to the Dublin Trio to join her.

So, the Trio made his way down to join her. Once he met this woman, and after they started talking, he realized she was very wise, and they had the most wonderful conversation. She has a cabin that's not far from the valley, and she said she grew up in that cabin. She told the Dublin Trio that long ago, the Gray Hawk Indians and the U.S. Cavalry had a fierce fight in this valley in the 1800s. This wise woman said that they fought for a few days but came to a mutual understanding with an exchange of mutual respect between them, despite their differing lifestyles. They both went their separate ways. After about an hour of talking with this wise woman, the Dublin Trio and the woman departed.

The Trio continued down this path along this valley, until he saw what he thought looked like an arrow lying in the brush alongside the path. So, the Dublin trio investigated it, and sure enough, it was an arrow. In addition, to his astonishment, he found a hatchet next to the arrow. He picked up the hatchet, and it had some markings on it. Then, the Dublin Trio tried to imagine the fearsome battle that broke out between the U.S. Cavalry and the Indians back in this valley in the 1800s.

The Dublin trio took the hatchet to a Native American historian to try to interpret the markings on the hatchet. The historian took the hatchet behind his curtain in his shop to examine it more closely. He became agitated as to how this person, who wasn't a Native American and had no idea of the Native American culture, could come in contact with such a relic of this nature, and he became very hostile. So, he went back out and accused the Dublin Trio of trying to undermine the Native American history and culture with this relic, since the historian feels it belongs in the hands of the Native American. He started gesturing at the Dublin Trio, as if he wanted to fight them. The Dublin Trio wasn't going to back down from a confrontation, especially if he knew he was in the right. So, the Native American historian and the Dublin Trio step outside.

"Let's settle this, then," said the Trio, his voice was a low hum, like a distant drumbeat. "Away from the musty archives and the judgmental stares of ancient spirits."

The Dublin Trio, in a blur of motion, bowed with a flourish. His eyes, sharp and glinting, scanned the space.

"Ah, a private audience with history itself," the historian said.

A high-pitched laugh, almost a cackle, escaped the Trio's lips, echoing off the brick wall of the building.

"Finally, a stage worthy of true artistry!" The Trio said.

The Native American historian shifted his weight, his feet finding their place on the uneven ground. He wore leather moccasins and was as silent as a shadow. His stance was rooted, like an ancient cedar. No unnecessary movements, just coiled power.

"You speak of artistry," the historian rumbled, his gaze steady. "I speak of purpose."

"Purpose? My dear fellow, our purpose is to demonstrate the exquisite precision of the human form!" The Trio replied. His hands, lightning fast, blurred into a series of open-palm strikes, slicing through the air with a faint *whoosh*.

"The dance of disciplined power!" said the historian. He watched, unblinking. He didn't flinch, didn't react, just absorbed the performance. Then, with a subtle shift, he lowered his chin. "Show me your dance, then."

The air crackled. The Dublin Trio, suddenly serious, dropped into a low crouch, their muscles coiling like springs. He moved first, a sudden burst of speed. *Thwack!* A kick, aimed low, whistled past the Native American historian's knee. He swayed, almost imperceptibly, avoiding the strike with the grace of a willow in a storm.

The Trio spun like a whirlwind, delivering a rapid succession of punches, each one aimed at a pressure point. *Whiz! Pop!* The Native American historian, a master of deflection, parried with forearms, absorbing blows with surprising softness, redirecting energy rather than opposing it.

"A-ha!" The Trio grunted, frustration creeping into their voice. "Nimble, aren't we?" The Native American historian didn't reply; his movements were fluid, economical. He moved like water, flowing around the Trio's rigid strikes. Then, seeing an opening, the Trio launched himself forward, a blur of white. He ran, a sudden sprint, and sprang into the air, a gravity-defying leap. His legs, strong and lean, wrapped around the Native American historian's throat in a scissor lock, a perfect, inescapable hold.

"Urgh!" A strangled gasp escaped the Native American historian as the world tilted. The Trio's weight, concentrated and heavy, bore down. His grip tightened, relentless.

"Gotcha!" the Trio wheezed, strain evident in his voice. "Now, what was that about purpose, eh?"

The Native American historian swayed, his eyes wide. The asphalt spun. He was strong, but the sudden, concentrated weight and crushing pressure on his windpipe were overwhelming. His knees buckled. A low moan, a guttural sound of effort and pain, escaped him. The world spun faster. The Trio was top-heavy, off-balance. *CRUMPH!* The Native American historian collapsed backward, a dead weight, taking the Dublin Trio with him, his grip still locked around his throat as they hit the unforgiving ground.

"Alright, my friend, let's move on beyond this point peacefully as our forefathers did." The Dublin Trio said as he helped the Native American historian up off the ground and told him, "I have a lot of respect for the Native American culture, especially your culture's deep respect and connection with the natural world. Also, I admire how your culture reveres its elders for their wisdom and experience gained through living and overcoming adversity, as well as maintaining balance with oneself. Let me give you my silver star, which was given to me for my courage and valor. I want to give it as a peace offering from me and you. I can get another one, so don't worry about me, but I want you to have this as a token of peace between you and me."

Both men shook hands, and all significant picture concepts come to fruition from small seeds that are planted. The lesson here is that outstanding accomplishments start with small steps.

Messages from Beyond

The Dublin Trio is traveling southbound on Interstate-95, heading out of Philadelphia, when he sees a bad car accident where a man was thrown from a vehicle. By the time the Trio reached him, a crowd of bystanders gathered, their faces painted with a mix of shock and morbid curiosity. Near the wreckage, a figure lay motionless. He'd been thrown from the car on impact, and now his body was in broken shape in the grass. His breath was a shallow, gurgling rattle.

The Trio saw a glazed, vacant look in the man's eyes, a look that spoke to a consciousness on the edge of fading forever. The Dublin Trio started to resuscitate him using CPR techniques he learned in the military. To the Dublin Trio's surprise, he started to feel the man's pulse grow stronger and his heart begin to revive. The Dublin Trio continued with the CPR until the man's heart was beating on its own.

A woman interrupted the Dublin Trio. She identified herself as a nurse practitioner and offered her assistance. She pulled her stethoscope out of her purse, took readings, and informed the Dublin Trio that his heart was getting stronger. Then suddenly the man opened his eyes and said, "I was told that wasn't my time yet, and the next thing I remember is waking up just now." The Dublin Trio asked him if he remembered anything else.

"I remember floating out of my body, encountering a beautiful light," he said. "I experienced a profound sense of peace and love. While I was having a life review, I sensed the presence of a powerful spiritual being, and he communicated with me. That being said, 'I have a message for the man who resuscitated you.' Within a second, I knew everything I needed to know to relay the information I had for you."

The nurse interrupts and says, "We'll get to that soon. Right now, you need rest." In the meantime, the Dublin Trio was perplexed and full of wonder as to what message could come from beyond. He has a strong feeling that this man had an afterlife experience that brought him close to God. The Trio remembers that initial contact he had with God in Tookany Park, and he figures the message must be of grave importance.

He needs to find out what his next mission is, so he visits the man in the hospital and they talk. The man who had the near-death experience was frightened as he spoke to the Trio.

"A third Antichrist has arrived," he began. "The first one being Napoleon, the second one being Hitler, and it's your job to confront the third Antichrist and undo his ambitious plans. Still, be aware of his deceitful charm and manipulation. He is well-crafted in the art of communication, and you can find him currently as a senator in the United States Senate, serving the state of Ohio." The Dublin Trio took this mission seriously, which was guided from above. He also felt trepidation due to the potential impact and outcome of his actions.

The Dublin Trio arrives home and readies itself for travel to Ohio to meet the senator. He visits the senator's contact page on the senator's website and requests an appointment to discuss some issues with the senator. Of course, his primary focus is to meet the senator and engage him. The senator's name is Phil Wilcox. An appointment was made, and the Dublin Trio walked into Senator Wilcox's office and sat down. This senator is polite and engaging, and asks the Dublin Trio what he can do for him. Still, the Dublin Trio is not here to match wits with the senator, and the Dublin Trio simply says, "I know who you are," which took the senator by surprise.

The senator was caught off guard initially, but he quickly adjusted and said, "What exactly are you referring to?"

"You want to play that game with me because I know the truth," said the Dublin Trio.

"What is your background again?" asked Senator Wilcox.

"I am a retired three-tour Green Beret officer who won the silver star, and I'm here to take you down," replied the Dublin Trio.

The senator was now moving more cautiously and awkwardly trying to adjust because he suspected that the Dublin Trio might know who he was. With grace and charm, he says, "I would like to thank you on behalf of the United States government for your service to our country."

"It would be more fulfilling when I bring you down with all your evil intentions," said the Dublin Trio.

The senator, who is starting to look more pensive and agitated, says, "What did you come in for today again, and how can I help you?"

"You can help by stopping lying to me, because I have the authority from above to bring you down," said the Dublin Trio.

The senator is now getting fed up with the Dublin Trio and says, "You don't scare me, you don't know what you're dealing with."

"It is you who is mistaken on the genuine, authentic powers of the universe, which in itself can stop you and crush you," said the Dublin Trio. "I'm here to help facilitate that to ensure that your evil is stomped out. Many powers are so much superior to you. I can only imagine your perception of power. You may think that the majesty of God's beautiful forest is harmless, but trust me, unraveling the universe's nature is enough to crush you in itself. I can demonstrate this superiority to you, if you let me, because I wanna show you the awesomeness of God's universe."

"You're going to show me that nature is superior to me?" said the senator incredulously.

"Absolutely, there's a State Park not too far from here," said the Dublin Trio, "I would like to demonstrate how nature is so much more superior to you and your misperception of power."

Both of them agreed to go to Mason State Park, which is not too far from the senator's office. The senator didn't believe what the Dublin Trio said about nature being superior to his evil energy. So, they both went into the park, and the Trio started saying, "The majesties of God's beautiful nature refer to the elements of the natural world that reveal the power, creativity, and glory of the divine. This can be observed in both the grand and the minute, in the immense power of the universe and in this subtle complexity of life on earth. For many, this observation evokes a sense of awe and reverence for the creator and this power. There are many divine powers under God's creation, but this element of the power of nature is so superior to your perception of power that you believe in."

"You know, I'm getting sick and tired of you lecturing me," said Senator Wilcox. "I happen to have a black belt in Karate. You have such a big mouth, but can you back up your words with your actions?"

The senator starts to take off his jacket and shirt, so he can fight at his highest peak.

"Black belt in Karate, huh?" The Dublin Trio replied. "Let's test your skills against a black belt in Kung Fu, and we'll see who prevails."

The senator didn't know he was up against such a worthy competitor, and the cockiness left his face as both of them squared off in the clearing in the park. In the heart of a sprawling state park, where the sun filtered through the leaves and the air was thick with the scent of pine, an unusual showdown was about to unfold. The Dublin Trio, a man of skilled martial artists known for his fluid movements and strategic prowess, faced off against a formidable opponent: Senator Wilcox, who was the Antichrist himself. His reputation for cunning and ruthlessness preceded him, but today, he would meet his match.

As the clearing echoed with the sounds of nature, the tension between the two sides was palpable. The Trio stood poised in his stance, his eyes locked on the Senator. With a swift nod, the battle commenced.

The Senator launched forward, his fists flying with a mix of karate precision and raw power. He aimed with a roundhouse kick, which the Trio sidestepped, countering with a series of quick jabs. The fight escalated, each side exchanging blows and showcasing their unique styles. The Senator's strikes were fierce, but the Trio's synergy was undeniable. They moved as one, anticipating each other's moves and covering each other's weaknesses. Just when it seemed the Senator might gain the upper hand, the Dublin Trio executed a surprise Kung Fu maneuver, sweeping low to catch the Senator off guard.

In an instant, Senator Wilcox found himself ensnared in a death grip, his arms pinned and his breath escaping him. The Trio had seized the moment; his training culminated in this decisive move. The Senator struggled, but the grip was unyielding, and defeat washed over him like a cold wave. The Dublin Trio left him on the ground, gasping for air, because the Trio felt he had made his point, and as the Trio walked away, the Antichrist, filled with vile evil, was not going to let this stand. As the Dublin Trio continued to walk away, the senator pulled out his switchblade and planned to stab the Dublin trail from behind. The Antichrist gathered himself, pulled himself erect, and started to catch up to the Dublin Trio. God, who sees all things, at all times, and commissioned the Dublin Trio on this mission, knew that the Dublin Trio was going to be stabbed from behind. So, God sent the Archangel Michael to intercede on the Dublin Trio's behalf. An angel wing that was transparent but was filled with white particles instantly separated the Dublin Trio from the Antichrist.

The Archangel Michael, with all his Godly abilities, made the Senator drop his switchblade, and the Antichrist, who knew who the angel was, fell to his knees. Archangel Michael said to him, "You have been given mercy, and you turned into evil. Did you really think we were going to let you carry out your plans on earth? We're going to let you continue in your capacity, but we want you to be an agent of God now. This is how the majesty of God's kingdom works: He demonstrates judgments on the sinners, but once they are converted, they can be his biggest advocates. You have been given a second chance. Never turn to evil again, for God's power is everlasting and inexhaustible."

The Dublin Trio walked out of the park with all of nature's splendors, and the birds were singing triumphantly as a new day was preserved in the pursuit of humans' journey.

Let Freedom Ring

Dublin Trio is at his neighborhood supermarket, and he hears the words "Code Red" announced on the public address system. He sees most of the staff walk to the front of the store at a hurried pace. The Dublin Trio became curious, and he went up to the front of the store. There, he saw a woman in a heated argument with the cashier over insufficient funds on her State Funded Access Card.

The woman was arguing with the cashier because she didn't want to put her groceries back. The woman in question made a phone call, and soon after, a mysterious, well-dressed man appeared and began representing her. He was a good talker, and the Dublin Trio could see that the guy in the suit was manipulating the situation to their favor. The Trio knew in his heart that he couldn't let this smooth talker succeed with his talking points.

Therefore, the Trio injects himself into the conversation and starts matching wits with the guy in the suit on behalf of the supermarket. Suddenly, the woman in question dropped her purse, and a few things came out. The Dublin Trio kneels to try to help her gather things. One of the items was an FBI Top Ten Most Wanted list, and the Trio saw her picture on the list. Still, the Trio was willing to stay cool in the moment and knew that if you're patient, time has a way of unraveling things. So, the Dublin Trio decided to follow her home. Once the Trio knew where she lived, he decided to come back with his nunchaku, which are two sticks connected by a short chain, and do some surveillance. He waits for everyone to leave, so he can break in and look around the house. Once the area was clear, the Dublin Trio opened a window from the back deck, entered the house, and started to look around.

He found in one drawer documents that she was a part of a terrorist cell that was planning an assassination attempt on the President of the United States when he was going to visit Independence Hall in Philadelphia to make a speech. Initial reports were that speech would be about the complex and often contradictory lives the leaders of the American Revolution led, because the President didn't want them to be criticized for living in a time that allowed for slavery. Instead, the President sought to foster an understanding of the era in which they lived. Although they were imperfect, they made brilliant contributions to the nation's founding.

As the Dublin Trio was leaving the house, two thugs saw the Trio leaving the house. The Dublin Trio clutched the rolled-up blueprints for this monstrous act tight against his chest. He cleared the back door, stepping onto overgrown grass, the scent of damp earth and rotting leaves thick in his nostrils. The fence loomed ahead, a dark, skeletal barrier against the moonless sky. A shadow detached itself from the deeper gloom near the tool shed. Then came another. Two hulking forms, their silhouettes distorted by the insufficient light. The first man, a barrel-chested brute, swung a baseball bat low, the wood catching a glint of the distant streetlamp.

"Where do you think you're going, rat?" The voice rumbled, low and menacing.

Dublin Trio stopped, his breath held. He didn't reply, his fingers already unhooking the nunchaku from his belt. The heavy chain clinked softly, a metallic whisper in the stillness.

"He's got something," the second man barked, his voice higher, sharper. He hefted a heavier, splintered piece of lumber. "Look at him, trying to sneak off with our plans."

"Plans for what?" Dublin Trio asked. His voice was calm, almost conversational, belying the tension coiling in his gut.

"You know damn well for what," the first man snarled, taking another step forward. His eyes, which looked like dark pits in the dim light, narrowed. "The President. You thought you could walk out with our work?"

The nunchaku spun, a blur of wood and chain, a faint *whoosh* cutting the silence. The first man flinched, his bat rising instinctively.

"You're going to regret that," he spat, charging forward. His swing was wide, powerful, but telegraphed. Dublin Trio dipped, the bat whistling over his head, a gust of displaced air brushing his hair. The nunchaku snapped back, the end of one stick cracking against the man's elbow. A sharp cry, a yelp of pain, tore from him. The bat clattered to the ground.

The second man, fueled by rage, moved in. "You think you're tough?" he yelled, his bat arcing down in a clumsy overhead strike. Dublin Trio met it not with a block, but with a swift, upward thrust of his nunchaku, catching the bat's shaft. The impact jarred the man's hands, a dull thud resonating. Before the man could recover, the Dublin Trio spun, the chain wrapping around the bat, wrenching it from his grip with a sharp *thwack*. The bat flew into the darkness, landing with a distant clatter. The first man, cradling his arm, rushed back in, throwing a wild punch. The Dublin Trio ducked under it, a fluid motion, then brought the nunchaku up, the wooden stick striking the man's ribs with a dull *crack*. A guttural gasp escaped him. The man stumbled back, clutching his side, his face contorted in agony.

"This is your last chance," the second man rasped, his fists balled, raw anger contorting his features. He lunged, a desperate, untrained charge. The Dublin Trio sidestepped, a blur of motion. As the man stumbled past, the Dublin Trio pivoted, bringing the nunchaku around in a tight, controlled arc. The wood was connected to the back of the man's knee. A sickening *pop* followed by a scream. The man's leg buckled, sending him crashing to the ground, a desperate moan escaping his lips. The first man, still clutching his ribs, watched his partner fall. His bravado evaporated, replaced by a raw, naked fear. He backed away slowly, his eyes wide and unfocused.

"Stay down," the Dublin Trio commanded, his voice low, a quiet authority echoing in the night. He glanced at the rolled-up plans, still secure in his grasp. The silence of the backyard settled once more, broken only by the ragged breathing of the two defeated men and the distant city hum. The Dublin Trio walked away with the plans to assassinate the President when he visits Philadelphia.

The Dublin Trio turned over the plans to the FBI so they could make the necessary arrests. We must remember our forefathers, who paid the price for our freedom. So, let the cry call out from sea to shining sea and let freedom ring.

In the ensuing months, the team of officials who were planning the President's arrival in Philadelphia surprised The Dublin Trio by inviting him to the ceremony in front of Independence Hall, and the President wanted to award The Dublin Trio the Medal of Freedom for his bravery in breaking up that terrorist cell to assassinate him.

So, the Dublin Trio goes up to the stage to accept his Metal of Freedom Award and gives this speech: "I would like to start by thanking the President for this highly esteemed honor. I want to dedicate this speech to all the teenagers who are trying to navigate through their teenage years, because those years are the most impressionable for our teenagers. Let's talk about leadership when you are under the influence of peer pressure. You have to be strong, follow your heart, use good judgment, and let your heart guide you because those values will be your greatest compass. You will be tested if you don't follow the crowd, but charting your own path also has many character-building skills, as you build momentum into adulthood. Rely on your faith as you walk down that path. Good luck!"

Excalibur for a New Day

The Dublin Trio was in Nevada sightseeing and had scheduled a skydiving outing to revisit his days as a Green Beret. While en route to the airfield where he would do his skydiving, he fell asleep at the wheel; his car drifted and wandered down a dirt road. He went through a barricade, which woke him up, and the next thing he knew, he was driving off the Grand Canyon.

As his car descended, the Trio reached for his parachute, but as it went down the canyon, he felt as if the vehicle was being suspended in mid-air. All of a sudden, a voice came over his car radio speaker and said, "I am Archangel Gabriel, messenger angel of God, and I bring a message of a new dawn."

The Archangel explained that humanity was at a critical point, with its future uncertain. The path forward required a shift in collective consciousness, rather than technological progress or political strategies. A new spiritual leader is needed to guide this change. Archangel Gabriel explained that a sword, similar to Excalibur, was set in stone. This stone was in the foothills of North Carolina, in the town of

Blowing Rock, but few knew about it. Ryan Shamus was one of three people asked to try to remove the sword from the stone. The Archangel said that the sword had spiritual meaning, since the sword was not a weapon, but an instrument of peace. It would not grant worldly power, but would be a guide for humanity's spiritual progress, the start of a new age. The Archangel went on to say that the sword could not be obtained through force. Instead, it would yield to the right person with the right qualities for new-age leadership. These qualities include courage from compassion, resilience from inner peace, and a clearer understanding of humanity's darker side.

"Ryan, with your experience as a Green Beret, you possess these attributes," said Archangel Gabriel. "You will go to Blowing Rock with the other two men and attempt to pull out the sword." In the meantime, the Dublin Trio was aware that his car was descending slowly, and the Archangel Gabriel told the Dublin Trio to put on his parachute. The Trio did so, and within moments the car regained its regular speed of dissent, but the Dublin Trio was prepared. He maneuvered himself out of the vehicle and parachuted safely to the ground.

The Dublin Trio returned to his rented room and did some research on King Arthur from his laptop. What the Dublin Trio learned was that King Arthur's story is a legendary tale from medieval Britain, most likely based on a real British war leader who fought off invaders around the 5th and 6th centuries AD. In these stories, he is born to Uther Pendragon and Igraine, and later proves himself by pulling Excalibur from a stone. He establishes the Knights of the Round Table, the castle of Camelot, and leads a glorious reign marked by chivalry and the quest for the Holy Grail.

The Dublin Trio gathers his things and cuts short his trip to Nevada and heads to the hills of North Carolina looking for this New Age Excalibur Sword somewhere in the area of Blowing Rock, but how does he find it? The Dublin Trio, being inclined to create gadgets, started to think that he needed to build a device that would detect an energy resonance. If the rock from which the sword was emitting some energy, given its divine origin, this device would detect any electromagnetic fields. The Dublin Trio knew that there are online devices that he can order through the Internet that were created for health purposes. These sensors help collect data from your body for your well-being, but the Dublin Trio feels he can adjust these sensors to the atmospheric conditions to help him find the New Age Excalibur in the stone. They would help pick up an electrical signal if he rewired the system.

The Trio recalls that two other men were also selected to find the stone, and one of them will be chosen for this honorable assignment. So, the Dublin Trio ventured into the woods of Blowing Rock in search of the stone that supposedly holds Excalibur. He had a sensor that detected electromagnetic energy. It took him down a path, and he came upon a beautiful waterfall. The sensors told him he was very close to the stone, but there was no stone to be found. This mystified the Trio, so he took a closer look at the waterfall, and it looked like there was a clearing behind the waterfall. Therefore, the Dublin Trio walked to a ledge behind the waterfall and navigated behind it, where he found a clearing. In the middle of this clearing was the stone with the sword in it. The sword had a luminous glow to it. On a nearby bench was another man. He was waiting for the other two men to show up. This person was noble, or else Archangel Gabriel wouldn't have chosen him to begin with. After he was chosen, greed had entered his heart, and he wanted to do the mission for glory and recognition, not for the right intentions. So, when the Dublin Trio arrived, the man with the bad intentions engaged the Trio in conversation based on false pretenses and cunning. All the while, this man sought to lead humanity in new age spirituality teachings, driven by his own greed and desire for fortune.

When they were walking around the stone and the sword, analyzing it, the man with the bad intentions picked up a rock and hit the Dublin Trio over the head with it, knocking the Trio out. He thought he had a clear path to pulling out the sword, but fate was stronger. He struggled and heaved and hauled, but couldn't pull out the sword. When the Dublin Trio came to and saw him working, and said, "Excalibur will not come out for you! First of all, you have to be pure at heart to pull the sword out of the stone for such a noble mission. You took a blessing from God and turned it into greed for your own use, and that's why you can't pull out the sword from the stone."

"Did you not hear the words of Archangel Gabriel when he said the sword is a message of peace and compassion and is not a weapon of destruction?" The Trio continued. "You fool! Stop thinking you could fool around with the fabric of God's will."

The man in question was not in the mood to hear a lecture from the Dublin Trio. So, he pulled out the hunting knife hitched to his belt and came at the Dublin Trio, swinging the knife menacingly. The Dublin Trio had seen it all before, since he was a former Green Beret and was skilled in the martial arts. He quickly grabbed his arm with the hunting knife, flipped him, put his foot on his throat, and said, "I don't doubt that you weren't a noble man to be picked for this assignment, but you have to remember that when you're picked for an assignment like this, it is an honor to serve the Kingdom of God. You are not to think of yourself. Now pick yourself up and leave before I kick your ass!"

Shortly thereafter, the other man shows up. He and the Dublin Trio got into a serious contemplative discussion on the seriousness of what all this means, and whoever pulls out the sword must have the utmost serious mind and the most profound conviction, for such a responsibility. They both agree that the Dublin Trio should go next and attempt to pull out the sword. As the Dublin Trio put both hands on the sword, trepidation was evident in his thoughts. At the same time, he tried to compose himself, and when he pulled out the sword, it came out like it was in a piece of butter. He held it with honor, for it bestowed great responsibility.

Then a luminous figure, which had a winged shape, appeared and spoke to the Dublin Trio. The Trio recognized Archangel Gabriel, and he got down on one knee. The angel said to him, "You have served your country and now you're going to serve the kingdom of God." Next, the Archangel Gabriel picked up the sword and tapped each shoulder and said, "You are now a Knight and Ambassador on behalf of the Kingdom of God. You may rise, my son; you have a great deal of work that needs to be done. Your faith is strong, and that will always be your compass. Good luck."

The Dublin Trio turned to the other man and asked for his assistance in bringing in a new era of peace that would broaden people's minds about the immeasurable power of God. Both men emerged from behind the waterfall into a new day for humanity.

Daniel Boone and the Genie Lamp

Daniel Boone was an American pioneer and frontiersman whose exploits made him one of the first folk heroes of the United States. He became famous for his exploration and settlement of Kentucky, which was then beyond the western borders of the original 13 states. Stories of Daniel Boone include the capture and rescue of his daughter, Jemima Boone, as well as his own capture by the Shawnee Indians, during which he was adopted by Chief Blackfish and given the name Big Turtle. There was also his family's retreat after his son's death, his serving as a militia officer and legislator, and his eventual move to Missouri later in life.

One day, while on the Cumberland Gap Trail in Kentucky, Daniel Boone found shelter in a cave. There, he dug a pit to create a fire and discovered a lamp. It was an unusual-looking lamp, and as he studied it, a mist emerged from the lamp. From the fog emerged an 8-foot-tall, transparent genie. The genie spoke these words to Daniel Boone, "Thank you, esteemed master, you have released me from my ancient vessel. As is tradition and out of my boundless gratitude, I shall grant you three wishes, but let me first discuss my experiences with you. Throughout the ages, man has let me down, always seeking possessions and money rather than what truly matters: health and well-being. You can wish for whatever you want, but these are my thoughts, and I feel I should express them to you."

"I want to do the most responsible thing considering the circumstances, so I wish for good health," said Daniel Boone.

"It has been granted," replied the genie.

Daniel Boone reburied the genie lamp and placed a note around it with a rope knot to keep it in place. The note said this:

This is a genie lamp, and whoever discovers it will have three wishes granted. Please, don't be tempted to ask for material things or money. Instead, ask for things that will help you move forward, such as those grounded in a solid work ethic. This wish will never burn out and will always bring you many blessings throughout your life. Good Luck!
Daniel Boone

After burying the lamp, Daniel Boone went on to have a very successful life as one of America's most outstanding pioneers.

The genie then remained untouched until 2025, when a writer named William Woodsman wanted to do a biography of Daniel Boone. He tried to retrace the steps of Daniel Boone as he first saw Kentucky, which, by many accounts, was a very breathtaking moment in Boone's life. So, while Woodsman was following the trail of Daniel Boone through the Cumberland Gap, he sought shelter. It so happened that he went into the same cave as Boone. Once inside the cave, Woodman decided to dig for water, since he was very thirsty.

While digging for water, he found the genie lamp, with a note from Daniel Boone. He was thrilled to discover such a significant artifact, accompanied by a handwritten note from Boone. Before he knew it, a mist came out of the genie lamp, and the genie appeared before the Woodman and said, "I have granted kings their kingdoms and merchants their fortunes with their wishes. Most people who find me are looking for a conclusion to their journey. So, I have seen the end of many journeys. The true reward is not the destination, but in the path you walk."

"Genie, my wish is a humble one, and it's a wish for wisdom," said Woodsman. "I'm writing a biography on Daniel Boone, and he left a note attached to your lamp, so it looks like you had an encounter with him. If you could share some wisdom that would help me describe what kind of person he was, it would greatly benefit me."

"Behold! For millennia, mortals have risen and fallen, and their names are quickly forgotten," said the genie. "But the name of Daniel Boone, the wind respects that name. Most so-called heroes seek fortune or to defeat a great enemy. But what did Boone want? Nothing! He wanted to walk. And walk, he did. He did more than all the kings and conquerors combined. He was a wanderer of consequence. Many wander, but most are lost. Boone was different. He blazed the trail with his senses, courage, and determination. He paved a path in the wilderness for his generation to move westward."

With this in hand, Woodsman completed his journey, having compiled enough notes to complete his biography of Daniel Boone. He returned home to Rhode Island and began working on his biography of Daniel Boone. He began to reflect on Daniel Boone's bravery and wondered if anyone today would meet his level of leadership. He thought that maybe the Navy Seals or someone from a Special Ops unit would be a good candidate to interview to get a modern perspective and give his readers an equal playing field between the different generations.

So, Woodsman goes online in the hope of finding a civilian ex-special ops officer. He finds Ryan Shamus, a three-tour Green Beret officer who goes by the alias Dublin Trio, and assists those in need. Woodsman contacted him to interview the Trio, via video chat, for his book.

The arrangements were made for them to talk, and the interview took place. "Mr. Shamus, Daniel Boone demonstrated so much bravery and courage in pioneering and foraging forward and settling the wilderness beyond the original 13 states," said Woodsman. "He helped to settle Kentucky when he led pioneers through the Cumberland Gap. He became a legendary figure, embodying the spirit of the American frontier and influencing the westward expansion of the United States. How would you say your experience as a special OPS operative and Green Beret was related to Daniel Boone's experience?"

"I could never compare what we did in the military to the contribution of Daniel Boone," said the Dublin Trio. "I can discuss the values that we hold close to our hearts. Green Beret special officers are known for their unwavering commitment to a set of core values, which are emphasized throughout our training and career. These values, articulated in our creed and actions, reflect our dedication to the team, country, and mission. Green Berets are committed to the cause and have the mental and physical resolve to see the mission through, no matter the difficulty."

When Woodsman finished his interview with the Dublin Trio, he realized the virtues and the unselfish commitment that both the Trio and Daniel Boone had in common. Drawing a comparison between the virtues of Daniel Boone and modern Green Berets highlights a shared tradition of self-reliance and the ability to lead in remote, challenging environments, albeit within very different contexts. While Boone was an individualist frontiersman exploring the unknown, Green Berets are part of a highly trained, organized military unit with specific tactical, diplomatic, and ethical mandates. Woodsman concluded that the ability to adjust and overcome unexpected challenges with limited resources was a key trait for both.

A Woman's Cry

A surprise visitor arrived at the Dublin Trio's door. It was a woman and she was banging on his door with ferocity and panic, shaking the Dublin Trio out of his chair with urgency. He rushed to the door with curiosity. With a quick opening of the door, the woman leaped into his arms, and the Dublin Trio ushered her into the house. She yelled to him, "Quickly close the door", and the Dublin Trio had her sit in the chair.

Soon after the woman in question sat in the Dublin Trio's chair, the door knocked again with force. He answered the door to find two guys there, asking the Dublin Trio about the woman who had knocked a few moments ago. The woman in question, who was sitting in Dublin Trio's chair, begged him not to let the men in. The men at the door showed the Dublin Trio government-issued FBI credentials. They said they had a warrant for her arrest, and she needed to be questioned.

The Dublin Trio felt compelled to let the men in and take the woman with them, despite her resistance as they were leaving. The Dublin Trio wanted to verify their credentials again due to the woman's resistance. The men showed their credentials again and the Dublin Trio took a picture of them with his cell phone. As he took a picture of their credentials, he noticed a look of discomfort on both men's faces and wondered what it was all about.

The Dublin Trio sat in his living room, pondering the situation, thinking, and speculating. As he did, he put his hand in his pocket and found a locker key. This is a key from the lockers at the Philadelphia airport. He thought that the woman in question must have planted this locker key into his pocket during their embrace, and this really perplexed the Dublin Trio. Why would she plant a locker key in his pocket? He feels compelled to look inside the locker, so he drove to Philadelphia International Airport.

Once there, he went to the locker, opened it, and found an FBI operative badge and credentials, and learned her name is Maureen O'Rourke. He also found a newspaper clipping with her picture. The clipping was an article about a big drug bust she was involved in when she was the head of a team of FBI agents. This led to one of the nation's most significant drug arrests against the Drug Cartel, and it resulted in Maureen, who was the head FBI operative, having to go on the Witness Protection Program. The Dublin Trio also found two newspaper clippings of him in the locker.

One notable instance was his retirement from the Army's Special Ops Unit, and another was his return home after completing three tours of duty. Now the Dublin Trio felt compelled to help this woman who was dragged out of his living room by two unidentified men with FBI credentials. Thankfully, he had the picture of the two men's credentials.

The Dublin Trio goes home, goes on the computer, and starts searching around, looking here and there, and learns that two FBI agents were murdered two weeks ago, in their car during a stakeout. So, the Dublin Trio conducted research and discovered where the vehicle was being compounded. He put on his nighttime stealth outfit and decided to jump the fence where the car was parked. It wasn't long after that a dog, a Rottweiler, ran out from a distance, and the Dublin Trio heard the pitter-patter of footprints from behind him. He knew he was going to be attacked from behind, so he turned to face his aggressor and said with urgency in his voice, "Come on!"

The Trio stood there waiting and knew that this was going to be a fight to the finish, but suddenly, the rottweiler stopped in his tracks. These dogs like to be the pursuer. When faced with fearlessness, they back down. The Dublin Trio prepared for the possibility of a security dog in the compound by bringing meat in his trousers, which he then gave to the Rottweiler, distracting it. The Dublin Trio found the car in question, where the two FBI agents were murdered, and started to investigate the vehicle. He scrutinized everything and found a hair follicle on the back of the driver's side seat. He picked it up with tweezers and placed it in a zip-lock bag that he had brought with him.

Once he arrived home, he shipped off the follicle to his connections in forensics and had to wait several days until his connections emailed him the results. In the meantime, he did more research on Maureen

O'Rourke and realized that it was no accident that she ended up knocking on his door for help. As he investigated her past, he learned she was a highly decorated child academic in space-time mechanics and won many state-wide all-around gymnastics competitions. He also found that at the age of 17, she was awarded one of the highest awards for bravery while camping with her family.

While walking on a trail, she noticed a child separated from her family. As the family realized their child was missing and returned to retrieve her, a grizzly bear emerged from the brush. The bear started to approach the child menacingly. Maureen instinctively put herself between the child and the danger. The grizzly bear bore down on Maureen with ferocity. Maureen was frightened, but stood her ground. All she had on her was a hunting knife. As Maureen was calculating the distance between her and the bear, she recalled her gymnastic days.

When the bear got within 10 feet of her, she took several steps forward, leaped into the air, did a somersault, and landed on the back of the grizzly bear. She put both her hands over the eyes of the bear, and it ferociously tried to dislodge Maureen by violently thrusting its neck and shoulders back and forth, but Maureen hung on. She knew what she had to do and pulled out her hunting knife, reached around to the front of the grizzly bear, and stabbed it in its throat several times. Slowly, the bear slowed his pace until he was resting with nature and peace, and Maureen picked up the child and returned her to her parents.

As the Dublin Trio read this newspaper clipping, he was in awe of Maureen O'Rourke's bravery. Next, she attended college to earn a degree in criminal justice. She then entered the FBI Academy and rose through the ranks at the bureau. He must find a way to save her.

The hair follicle results have come back, and now the Dublin Trio has a name and an address to go on. That night, the Dublin Trio went down to rescue Maureen. When he arrived at the location, he entered the home through the basement window. It was a pretty large home. Off in the distant air, he could hear Maureen's cries for help, but the Dublin Trio had to be cautious, as he was in an area he wasn't too familiar with. He proceeded with caution, entering a portion of the house that resembled a house of mirrors, which proved very confusing to the Trio.

He tried to make sense of the passageway of the mirrors. The maddening thing was that the Trio kept hearing Maureen's cry for help. In the meantime, Maureen was suspended in a torture device, and every time she showed resistance or moved, she would get a painful shock of electricity. The Dublin Trio navigated through the mirrors and followed Maureen's cries to her location. He removed her from her torture device, and she just about leaped into the Dublin Trio's arms. They both navigated through the house and exited through the same window through which the Trio had come. Maureen O'Rourke reestablished herself with the FBI, where she feels she belongs.

This story reinforces the principle that with hard work and belief, your dreams can come true. When you trust yourself and put energy behind your beliefs, unbelievable things can happen for you because there is inexhaustible energy in hope.